# *Bingoed*

An Essie Cobb Senior Sleuth Mystery

by

Patricia Rockwell

For information, email **Cozy Cat Press**,
cozycatpress@aol.com or visit our website at:
www.cozycatpress.com

**COZY CAT**
**P R E S S**

ISBN: 978-0-9844795-7-3

Printed in the United States of America

Cover design by Atomic Werewolf Studio
www.atomicwerewolfstudio.com

PUBLISHER'S NOTE: The publisher is not responsible for any adverse reaction to eating any of the dishes created from the recipes contained in this book.

10 9 8 7 6 5 4 3 2 1

Dedicated to Dorothy, my favorite senior, and to her cat that faces north

# Chapter One

*"Growing old is mandatory; growing up is optional."*
—Chili Davis

"G-52!"

A room of grey and white-haired heads tipped down in unison as they perused their Bingo cards. At a square table covered with a white cloth sporting one lovely fake flower in a crystal vase, the wide eyes of Essie Cobb quickly scanned the Bingo cards before her. Then, seeing that none of her three cards (the most allowable at Happy Haven's Wednesday night Bingo games) sported the called-out letter-number combination, she quickly peeked over the tops of her glasses and gazed around the room to see if any of her competitors would beat her to a win. As no player apparently had a "52" in their "G" column, the caller selected another circular wooden piece from the wire bin.

"N-36," called out Sue Barber in a strong voice, glancing around the room as she waited for the senior players to check their cards.

This was Sue's second year as Happy Haven's Social Director. The job of Bingo caller was one of her primary duties—and she took it seriously. Once, early in her tenure when she had read off the numbers too rapidly, the residents had complained vociferously—and immediately. What did she take them for? Speed readers? After all, most of them had three cards they had to check (although it wasn't required that any player have three cards, their chances of winning increased—well—threefold—when they did. And to a one, the residents loved winning, even though the prize for winning a round of Bingo was only one dollar.) Sue reached carefully into the wire barrel again and pulled out another wooden tile.

"B-2," she sang out. This time her reading was rewarded as an elderly gentleman sitting close to the main door to the dining hall (where Bingo was always held) said in a somewhat wavering voice,

"Bingo!" The old gentleman rose carefully from his seat, as the women at his table (women outnumbered the men at Happy Haven about eight to one) cooed with admiration. He stood, still clutching the edge of the table with his gnarled hands, and smiled, nodding his chin at all of the women around him.

"Mr. Weiderley!" announced Sue Barber. "You have Bingo, Bob?" She started towards the man.

"Foo!" whispered Essie to her three tablemates. "I was just one space short in my B column!"

"I was one space short in B and G!" topped the tiny lady next to her, her bright eyes sparkling. "What about you, Opal?"

"What does it matter?" replied the tall, morose-looking, grey-haired compatriot to her right. "I never win at Bingo. You know that, Marjorie."

"Fay," said Marjorie to the plump woman seated to her other side in a wheelchair, "Fay, wake up. Bob Weiderley just got Bingo." She poked the woman, who sputtered and opened her eyes.

"What? What?" she tittered. "What happened?"

"Bob won Bingo," reiterated Essie to the group. Chubby-cheeked Fay considered the information for a moment, and then allowed her head to plop back on her shoulder.

"I hate to lose, but if I have to lose, I can't imagine losing to a nicer person," continued Essie.

"You just say that, Essie, because you have a crush on Bob," said Marjorie. Her head of tight reddish grey curls neatly hugged her skull like an aviator cap.

"Maude's cods!" scoffed Essie. "I'm too old for him. He's only 82."

While the four women argued, Sue Barber had finished checking Bob Weiderley's Bingo card for accuracy and had evidently found it all correct.

"Ladies and gentlemen," she called out as she strode to the center of the room, her canvas apron flapping as she walked. All heads turned to their Social Director. "Bob's card appears to be accurate. I am delighted to award him this $1.00 prize!" She reached into a front pocket of her apron and pulled out a crisp new bill, held it up high for all to see, and then handed it out in Bob Weiderley's direction with great ceremony.

"Hmmph," snorted Opal. "Have you noticed how more men seem to win Bingo ever since Sue Barber became our Social Director?"

"What?" asked Essie, pushing her round glasses back up her pointed little nose. "That's impossible! First of all, there's no way men could ever do anything more than women here because we outnumber them . . . "

"Eight to one," answered Opal and Marjorie together. Fay had again fallen asleep and was snoring gently in her wheelchair, her head resting on the collar of her fluffy pink lace blouse.

Bob Weiderley scooted to the center of the room, leaning on his three-footed cane. He reached out to accept the dollar bill from Sue Barber with a tentative smile. Sue held the bill in the air, showing his prize to the entire room.

"I see that Bob is all full of himself," added Opal under her breath. "Just look at that. You'd think he'd just won the Olympics instead of a Bingo prize."

"Hazel's basil!" responded Essie with such force that her lower dentures almost came loose. "Opal, if my memory serves me . . ."

"And it hardly ever does," opined Opal, giving Essie what Essie called her pretentious glare.

"If," continued Essie, scowling ferociously at her pal, "my memory serves me correctly, Opal—you won a Bingo round last week and when you won that dollar you'd think they'd crowned you Miss America!"

"Oh, Essie," interrupted Marjorie, poking Essie on her arm so hard it hurt, "technically, Opal couldn't win the Miss America contest which is only for unmarried women and we all know that she was married once upon a time."

"Who got married?" asked Fay the sleepyhead, suddenly aroused from her slumber. "Who got married?"

"No one, Fay," answered Marjorie, bending over her wheelchair-bound buddy and giving her head a gentle pat. "Bob Weiderley just won Bingo."  Fay considered this piece of information for a moment then drifted back asleep.

"It doesn't matter," said Essie.  "The point is that Bob is a dear and no one deserves to win Bingo more than he does."

"Absolutely," agreed Marjorie.  "I'm so happy for him!"  She shook her shoulders with enthusiasm and pulled down her sweater. Essie always disliked this mannerism because she believed Marjorie used it to call attention to her figure, which was actually fairly good for a woman of 84.

"You're both ridiculous," whispered Opal with disdain to the two awake women.  Then she leaned back in her chair and glanced back at the ceremony taking place in the center of the room.  Bob Weiderley was still accepting the accolades from his friends.  All of a sudden, as the women at Essie's table looked on from a distance, Bob Weiderley slumped to the floor.  Several women screamed.

"Oh, my!" shouted Sue Barber.  "Call the duty nurse!  Someone get Violet!"

An attendant dressed in a white jacket who had been standing watch quickly exited the main entrance to the dining hall as Sue Barber knelt beside the prone Bob Weiderley.  Residents started to gather around the man on the ground and Sue attempted to wave them back as she began loosening Bob's shirt collar and placing her ear to his mouth.

"Does he have heart trouble?" asked Marjorie.

"Everybody has heart trouble at that age," responded Essie.

"I don't," added Opal.  "My heart is in excellent condition, according to my cardiologist."

"If your heart's in excellent condition," said Marjorie, "why do you need a cardiologist?" Opal huffed.

"Please, you two," whispered Essie to her friends. "This is no time to bicker. Bob is sick."

"Should we do something?" asked Marjorie.

"I say the best thing we can do," responded Essie, "is to stay right here and do nothing until they tell us to do something."

"That's what we always do," retorted Marjorie.

"We might as well go to our rooms," suggested Opal. "After all, they probably won't continue with Bingo now that this has happened."

"Opal!" said Essie, aghast. "Let's just stay out of the way. "

Within seconds, Violet Hendrickson, the Director of the Happy Haven Assisted Living Facility, arrived at the scene along with Mildred, the night duty nurse. Mildred quickly bent down and conducted a cursory examination of Bob Weiderley. Then she spoke quietly to the Happy Haven Director, who turned and addressed the group.

"Residents," Violet announced. "We have an ambulance coming for Bob—Mr. Weiderley. I'd appreciate it if you'd all remain in your seats until the ambulance has taken Bob to the hospital. Then you all may return to your apartments. I'm certainly sorry for this disruption to Bingo night but I know you all are concerned about Bob and we will keep you updated on his condition."

With that, Violet Hendrickson, a slender, dark-haired elegant woman, slipped out of the room. The nurse Mildred and Sue Barber continued their vigil with Bob Weiderley. Sue held his hand while Mildred continued to check his vitals.

"Do you think it's his heart?" asked Marjorie.

"I don't know," answered Essie. "I just wish he had family. There's no one to call."

"I know," said Marjorie, "he's all alone. Poor Bob."

"He's lucky, if you ask me," interjected Opal with a sneer.

"Now what does that mean, Opal?" asked Marjorie in a confrontational manner.

"It means that far too many of the residents here have relatives who cause more trouble than they're worth!"

"That's ridiculous!" responded Essie. "Where do you get these ideas, Opal? I, for one, appreciate my family. Marjorie loves her relatives. And Opal, your daughter is lovely! What a delightful woman."

"Hmmm," said Opal with a downward inflection.

"For the love of Leonard, what's wrong with your daughter?"

"Nothing. Nothing," said Opal. "But just because the three of us have tolerable kin doesn't mean that everyone who lives here gets along with theirs."

"Why do you say the three of us? What about Fay?"

"Fay," whispered Opal, "is oblivious to the—adventures—of her, uh, children."

"What are you talking about, Opal?"

But before Opal could explain her words further, two EMTs arrived with a rolling gurney. They quickly relieved the nurse and Social Director Sue Barber from their posts beside Bob Weiderley. The men kneeled next to the man and began attaching various tubes and devices to his body. One EMT rolled a blood pressure cuff around Bob's arm and pumped it up and began to record his bp readings. The residents of Happy Haven watched in awed silence as the men worked quickly and quietly on their unconscious friend.

"So who gets the dollar?" asked Opal.

"What?" responded Essie.

"Who gets the dollar Bob won?" continued Opal. "He won't need it."

"Good Groundhog, Opal!" said Essie. "How can you think about such a thing with the poor man lying there on the floor?"

"He's not lying there anymore," said Opal. "He's on the gurney."

And indeed Bob Weiderley had been transferred by the efficient EMTs to the rolling gurney and was at that moment being pushed from the dining hall. Essie and her tablemates and all of the other residents maintained a respectful silence until the medical entourage had disappeared.   Then they erupted in a whirlwind of chattering.

"I hope they get him to the hospital in time," said Marjorie breathlessly.

"Lucky for him, the hospital's only two blocks away," added Opal.

"Do you think he'll be. . . okay?" queried Marjorie.

"I hope so," answered Essie.

"What do you think caused him to pass out?" asked Marjorie.

"I guess winning Bingo was just too exciting," suggested Essie. The three women looked back and forth at each other.

"I guess if you have to go, winning at Bingo is the best way," offered Marjorie.

"I can think of a few better ways," said Opal.

"Such as?" asked Essie, glancing sideways at her straight-laced and somber friend.

"Never mind," said Opal, shaking her head.  "He's not dead yet. Let's be positive."

"Yes," agreed Essie.

"Yes," said Marjorie.

All of a sudden, the pudgy short lady in the wheelchair awakened with a start.

"Bingo!" she yelled out loud and clear.

Her tablemates looked at her incredulously and then at each other, trying to subdue their inappropriate laughter.

## Chapter Two

*"Old age ain't no place for sissies."*
—Bette Davis

"Rise and shine, Miss Essie," called out a cheery voice.

Essie Cobb cautiously lifted one eye lid. Realizing that she was safely in her bed and that sunlight was streaming through her bedroom blinds, she ventured opening the second lid. As she glanced around, she saw the familiar face of her daily caregiver nurse, DeeDee Pritoni, hovering over her bed.

"It's after seven, Miss Essie," sang out DeeDee in her typical singsong voice. "We don't want to be late for breakfast now, do we?" She handed Essie her wire-rimmed glasses.

"I'm never late for breakfast," retorted Essie, slipping on her spectacles.

"You have a healthy appetite for sure!" chortled DeeDee, pulling Essie's comforter down and dragging her legs to the side of the bed.

"Let's get these socks on!" sang out DeeDee, her black pony tail swaying. She held up a pair of gym socks that she'd retrieved from Essie's drawers. Kneeling down, she quickly slipped them onto Essie's bare feet. Immediately following, she produced a pair of cotton briefs and quickly rolled them over the socks and up Essie's legs. Essie stood gingerly on the floor and began to hike up the pants. As the final step in underwear donning, DeeDee grabbed Essie's all-purpose bra from where Essie kept it, hanging around the bedroom door handle (in case she had to get ready fast during the middle of the night for a fire drill). Essie bent forward like a football player ready to tackle, arms slung forward as DeeDee pulled the bra on. Essie then tucked each cup with plentiful amounts of bosom flesh just as if she were stuffing a pillow. DeeDee completed the process by clipping the loosest three hooks on the back of the bra. Straightening up, Essie arranged her bosom around inside the cups—lifting, twisting, and pulling until her chest acquired the appropriate look and feel that she wanted.

"DeeDee," Essie said finally as her slim, sprightly aide headed for the bedroom closet. "Do you know how Bob Weiderley is?"

"I heard they took him to the hospital last night," yelled DeeDee from inside Essie's walk-in closet. "Shall we try these red trousers today, Essie?"

"No," replied Essie. "The brown ones."

"But you wore those yesterday," countered DeeDee, her melodious Italian accent almost inaudible with her head buried in a row of Essie's slacks and tops.

"And I want to wear them again," stated Essie firmly. DeeDee returned to the bedroom carrying the trousers in question.

"They're not very attractive," noted DeeDee with a lift of her neatly penciled eyebrow. She held up the pair of polyester pants as if they were a line of dead fish.

"But they're comfortable," responded Essie. End of discussion. "Do they know what happened to Bob?"

"Not that I know," said DeeDee, giving in and bending over to slip the trousers over Essie's feet. Essie assisted her by pulling up on the elasticized waistband. Then she stood up in her stocking-clad feet on her carpet so she could finish pulling on her favorite pants.

"You really should wear some of your other outfits, Essie. You have some lovely clothes. Goodness, if I had such beautiful blouses I would . . ."

"DeeDee," scowled Essie. "If you like my blouses so much you can have them. I don't need a closet full of clothes. I'm 90. I'm not a fashion model. Most of those things are too froufrou for me and way too uncomfortable! I don't know why my children insist on buying me so many clothes."

"Miss Essie! What are we going to do with you?" chided DeeDee as she held up two selections of tops from Essie's closet.

Essie pointed to the least colorful of the pair causing DeeDee to sigh.  Setting down the other top on Essie's dresser, she grabbed Essie's preferred top and bunched it up.  Essie, on cue, raised her arms and DeeDee slid the top over her head and down her body. "Now shoes!" commanded the shapely aide, hands on her hips. DeeDee grabbed Essie's sneakers from a chair beside her bed and when Essie sat back down on the bedside, DeeDee slipped them on the older woman's thin, tiny feet and tied the laces with an amazing speed.

"There we go!  Now we're all set!  Why don't we go sit down in our rocker while I get your meds ready?"

"Yes," said Essie, smiling.  "Why don't we sit in our rocker?  If we can both fit in it."

"Miss Essie," responded a laughing DeeDee.  "You make me laugh!"

"Too bad I can't make us both laugh since we tend to do everything together, don't we?" queried Essie.  She grabbed onto her red rolling walker which was stationed near the head of her bed and started to scoot into the small living room of her apartment. DeeDee followed her, turning immediately left into a kitchen nook where she unlocked a cabinet door above the sink.  She removed a rectangular plastic container and placed it on the counter.

"Surely someone here must know Bob's condition," mused Essie as she cautiously lowered herself into her favorite armchair, centrally located in her living room, with a writing desk on one side and a telephone table on the other.  Across the room, a television set stood in a place of honor.

"Violet must know," answered DeeDee, removing several pills from one of the square subdivisions of the pillbox.  She filled a glass with water at the sink and brought both pills and water over to the chair where Essie was now sitting.  "Here, our seven morning pills.  Bottoms up!"  She placed the pills in Essie's right palm and handed her the glass of water.  Essie took a cursory look at the pills, then plopped them all in her mouth at once and gulped them down with several swallows of water.  "I'm sure she'll tell the nurses on duty today what she knows. I mean, Bob's caregiver needs to know that he's not here."

"Did they take him to Fairview?" Essie asked.

"I guess so. That's where they take most residents because it's so close. Unless, of course, there's some reason the resident has requested a different hospital and I can't see any reason why Bob would do that."

"Poor Bob."

"Yes, such a nice gentleman."

"He doesn't have any family, does he?"

"I don't know." DeeDee had busied herself with putting away the pill container box and straightening up Essie's sink. "Now, Miss Essie, is there anything you need before I go?"

"No, I'll just sit here and work on my puzzles until breakfast."

"That sounds like a wonderful idea! I don't know how you ever manage to do those crosswords! I'm lucky if I can fill in two words," sang out DeeDee. "Have a great day!" She headed out Essie's front door into the hallway. Essie could see residents gliding back and forth outside of her doorway with their walkers, canes, and wheelchairs. It was like watching planes flying in a holding pattern around an airport, she often thought. All of the Happy Haven residents had their transportation machines of one sort or another and they all piloted them relatively well—some better than others.

DeeDee closed Essie's door and the sounds of the outside receded. Essie reached across her end table for her TV remote. She pushed the ON button and soon the sounds of a local news program filled her small apartment. She listened only briefly. She really wasn't much interested in news unless it was news about something going on at Happy Haven, because that was the focus of her world. She reached out again to her end table for a clipboard to which was attached a stack of puzzle sheets. She hadn't quite finished yesterday's puzzle. Quickly she became engrossed in pondering the remaining clues. She often spent the hour before breakfast working on her puzzles and most days she was able to complete one before she went for her morning meal.

As she scribbled some possible ideas in the puzzle squares, she considered the events of the previous evening. Why did Bob collapse? Was it a heart attack? Had he been sick? He always seemed perfectly healthy. Did they get him to the hospital in time? What about his family? Was it true that he had no one? No wife? No children? No one? How sad.

Most everyone she knew at Happy Haven had some family. Most of the women she knew well were widows but they all had children. Some even had children who lived nearby as hers did. Prudence and Claudia visited frequently and helped take care of things that she couldn't handle any longer such as her taxes and her bank account. Kurt wasn't so close, but he did visit from time to time. And, of course, there were the grandchildren. How many were there now? Seven? Eight? She couldn't quite remember. Let's see. One of them recently got married too. Which one was it?

She reached over to her desk on the other side of her armchair. Her hand touched her address book which she picked up and opened at random. In this book, she had recorded the names, addresses, and phone numbers of literally hundreds of people whom she had known through the years. As her eyes perused the page, she saw many names with a line drawn through them and a notation to the side indicating the status of the person. Most status indications that she added nowadays said "deceased." That is, most of the people who were no longer listed in her book had been removed because they had died. Soon, she thought, there won't be any names left in my book. Then, as quickly as the morbid thought had entered her mind, it left. Essie was not one to dwell on things she couldn't change. She was far more likely to think positively—or productively—as she coined it. If there was something wrong, why bemoan it? Why not figure out a way to make it right?

Another thought entered her mind. Again, it was about Bob Weiderley. Bob was worth thinking about, because as far as she knew, he was still alive. She determined to find out what she could about Bob and his condition. Also, she determined to find

out about his family—if he had a family.  And when Essie Cobb
determined to do something, she usually did it.

## Chapter Three

*"How does one keep from 'growing old inside'? Surely only in community. The only way to make friends with time is to stay friends with people."*
—Robert McAfee Brown

"Miss Essie, you like de nice omelets for breakfast?"

The young man in the white waiter's jacket stood patiently beside Essie, pencil poised.

"Yes, Santos, the omelets. And bacon. And, Santos, make sure they don't fry it to a crisp."

"Yes, Miss Essie," responded Santos, jotting down her directions. "And Miss Opal? Your regular?"

Opal nodded even though her head was still stuck in the covered leather menu that was provided to residents for all meals.

"Santos," interjected Marjorie before the young man had completed the previous diner's order. "I'd like some fresh fruit, please. What is fresh today?"

"Big strawberries, Miss Marjorie!" replied Santos, his eyes lighting up, his hands gesturing to indicate the size of the berries. "Huge! We make shortcake tonight. You have some this morning?"

"Yes," replied Marjorie, closing her menu and handing it to the waiter. "That's all I want. And, of course, some cream too." She smiled sweetly at the young man. *Just like she probably smiled at her first-graders when she taught elementary school*, thought Essie.

"What about Miss Fay?" asked Santos. "You think she want anything to eat?" Fay had drifted off in her wheelchair with her menu clutched against her chest.

"Just bring her a sweet roll," suggested Essie. "She can nibble on that when she wakes up."

"She'll just make a mess of that, Essie," said Opal with a slight sniff.

"She has to eat, Opal," argued Essie, "and besides, a sweet roll is probably the least messy item on the menu and she can take it with her if she doesn't finish it here." She smiled at Santos to indicate Fay's breakfast choice had been made.

"Yes, yes. Good, ladies," answered the cheerful young Latino. "I get breakfast. I be right back." He scampered off into the kitchen. Essie twisted around in her chair and glanced towards the dining hall door.

"What are you looking for?" asked Opal, stiffening to her full height of 5'9" in her chair. "Are you expecting someone?"

"No," whispered Essie. "I wanted to see if Bob was back."

"Essie," said Marjorie, "surely you wouldn't expect he'd be back so soon. They took him away in an ambulance last night! No one could make that quick of a recovery!"

"Have any of you heard anything about his condition?" continued Essie, looking at her companions, at least the two who were awake.

"My aide is Bob's aide too," contributed Opal. "She was told that he's in Fairview. She said he's in a coma."

"Oh no!" exclaimed Essie. The short tufts of scraggly white hair that grew where most people had eyebrows rose above the level of Essie's glasses.

"That's the last we'll see of him," Opal said dismally, her distress reflected in her sunken cheeks. "Remember last year ago when Edward Strott ended up in a coma. He was like that for weeks! Then he just died all of a sudden!" She heaved a sigh which was visible as a rolling movement in her entire upper torso from neck to waist.

"That doesn't mean that's what will happen to Bob," argued Marjorie in a sprightly voice. "People do come out of comas."

"I've heard that the longer they remain in a coma," said Essie, "the less chance they have of recovering." Her companions considered this observation for a moment.

"Then we just have to pray that he'll come out of it soon!" said Marjorie with a determined little punch of her fist and at the same time wiping her eye delicately with the corner of her table napkin.

"I just don't get it," said Essie, shaking her head. Her sparkling white locks gleaming in the morning sunlight belied her otherwise serious face.

"What don't you get, Essie?" asked Opal with a tilt of her simple, but neatly coifed head. "That old people get sick and die?"

"No," answered Essie, pursing her mouth into a wrinkled scowl. "Bob. Bob Weiderley. He's always seemed so healthy. Yes, he uses a cane, but have you seen him at exercise class?"

"You mean, have I seen him wearing his gym shorts and sneakers?" giggled Marjorie. "He does have a nice physique."

"That nice physique is just an indication of an athletic body," continued Essie. "Bob can do more push-ups than any other man at Happy Haven."

"That wouldn't be much of a challenge," noted Opal. She rolled her eyes, and lightly touched the namesake cameo around her neck.

"The point is, Opal, if you'll let me finish—the point is that Bob Weiderley is probably in better health than most. . ."

"A fine specimen of manhood," added Marjorie. She shimmied her shoulders suggestively.

"I just don't think he had a heart attack or stroke because he won a round of Bingo," claimed Essie. She folded her arms as if to indicate she was finished.

"Really, Essie," argued Opal, "at age 82, a man can have a heart attack or stroke just because. They don't need some instigating event like winning Bingo or running a mile or. . ."

"Having sex," suggested Marjorie sotto voce.

"Marjorie!" gasped Opal. "What would make you suggest that?"

"It's a possibility," responded Marjorie, her eyelids fluttering. "I wouldn't kick him out of bed for eating crackers!"

"Marjorie! Opal!" chimed in Essie. "Before you two come to blows, let me suggest that if Bob Weiderley were to die from sexual exertion, it would probably occur during the . . .uh, the . . . act itself—not during a round of Bingo." Marjorie and Opal both shrugged and Essie continued with her case. "No, I'm guessing that what we're looking at is some other event that caused Bob to collapse when he won that Bingo game last night."

"But what, Essie?" asked Marjorie.

"Yes, Essie, what?  Other than old age?" added Opal.

"That I intend to find out," replied Essie just as Santos returned with their breakfast plates in hand. He gracefully placed the dishes before each of the women.

"Breakfast is served, lovely ladies!" he announced. The women smiled and cooed at their regular breakfast fare. Santos accepted their responses, smiling and blushing, as if they were personal compliments.

"Santos, I have a question," said Essie, grabbing the young man's sleeve and pulling him close to her.

"Yes, Miss Essie," he responded gravely. "You change mind about bacon?" Marjorie and Opal dug into their food.

"No, no," she said, waving her hand. "I need to know about Bob Weiderley's table—over there." She gestured to the location by the main entrance where she knew Bob was assigned. "Do you know the three ladies who are Bob's tablemates?  I believe one of them is Hazel Brubaker, isn't she?"

"Yes, Miss Essie," replied the waiter, continuing to listen politely to the older woman. "Miss Hazel is the tall one and there's Miss Rose Lane and Miss Evelyn Cudahy. Mr. Bob; he is very nice gentleman.  We all very sorry he is ill."

"Which is Rose?"

"Miss Rose is the, the shorter . . . heavier lady with the bluish hair."

"And Evelyn must be . . ."

"Miss Evelyn is the one wearing the scarf.  She lose her hair from chemotherapy.  Poor lady.  Very nice."

"Thank you, Santos."

"Of course, Miss Essie.  I know you very nice lady.  You want to make Mr. Bob's table ladies feel better. "

"Yes, Santos," said Essie. Marjorie and Opal leaned in to hear her remarks to the waiter. "Yes, Santos, I want to speak to them and tell them how sorry I am about Bob."

"You very nice lady, Miss Essie," said Santos. Essie removed her palm from the young man's arm and smiled. Her table companions smiled benignly too and Santos headed off to the kitchen.

"You intend to pump those women for information, don't you, Essie?" demanded Opal.

"Pump is a very strong verb," said Essie, stabbing a lump of omelet with her fork.

"What do you think they can tell you about Bob, Essie, that you don't already know?" asked Marjorie. Her lips stopped in mid-air, poised around a large red strawberry.

Essie ignored Marjorie's question as she gobbled up a few bites of egg and bacon. Finally she spoke.

"If I run into them, I may offer my condolences," said Essie, wiping some bacon bits from her mouth.

"Condolences?" questioned Opal as she carefully nibbled at her soft-boiled egg, "Remember, he's not dead."

"Who's dead?" asked Fay, rousing from her wheelchair seat. Essie handed her the sweet roll on the plate before her. Fay sniffed it and then pulled off a small piece and plopped it in her mouth.

"No one, Fay," said Marjorie. "Bob is still alive as far as we know."

"Bob who?" asked Fay, totally engrossed in her sweet roll.

"Bob Weiderley," answered Opal. "He collapsed last night at Bingo."

"Where's the bacon?" asked Fay.

"Here," said Essie, handing Fay a piece of her bacon. "Have some of mine." Fay put down the sweet roll and began chomping on Essie's bacon.

"She doesn't eat bacon," noted Marjorie.

"She does today," said Essie, with a shrug. Then, bending conspiratorially towards her table mate, she asked, "Marjorie, are those three women still at their table?"

"You mean at Bob's table?" asked Marjorie.

"Yes; I don't want to turn around to look."

"They're all still there. Are you going over?"

"No, I'd rather talk to each one of them alone."

"Oh, I see," said Opal. "So they can't collude."

"So they can't collide?" Marjory asked Opal.

"No," explained Opal. "Essie's afraid that if she goes over there right now and talks to the women about Bob, they'll know what she's up to and they'll work together to keep her from getting information."

"You mean lie to her," added Marjorie. She bent so far towards Essie that one of her tight, little red curls flopped over her forehead. She quickly tucked it back into position.

"Maybe," said Essie. "Who knows? Maybe one of them is responsible for Bob's collapse at Bingo last night."

"Essie, you must be kidding!" snapped Opal. Her drawn, somber face looked even more imposing as she squeezed her eyebrows together and aimed her gaze straight at Essie. Opal had had a long, impressive career as an administrative assistant to a corporate lawyer. Over the years she obviously had polished her skills as a gatekeeper. One glance, one word from her was often enough to frighten off anyone who didn't know Opal as the basically gentle person she was.

"You never can tell, Opal," Essie maintained her argument. "That man was healthy. I just can't believe he collapsed and is now—in a coma!"

"Who's in a coma?" asked Fay, suddenly sitting upright, her eyes popping open.

"Never mind, Fay," said Opal. "Eat your bacon." Fay glanced down at the bacon slice hanging precariously from her chin. She immediately grabbed it and began to nibble.

"I don't suspect any of his tablemates," Essie said, as she slid her glasses up her nose, "but I do intend to talk to them to see what they know about Bob. What they know about his health."

"Why are you so interested in Bob all of a sudden, Essie?" asked Marjorie, wiping her mouth and folding her napkin.

"I just don't like to see anything bad happen to any of us here. We're all in the same boat, aren't we?  If I collapsed at Bingo, I hope the two of you would try to figure out why."

"Oh, Essie, you know we would!" exclaimed Marjorie.

"Speak for yourself," said Opal.  "I'm no detective."  She pushed her chair out from the table and slowly rose to a standing position behind her walker.  "I'm heading back to my room."

"We'll see you at lunch, Essie," said Marjorie, standing to join Opal.  She rolled her walker around and the two women pushed their personal vehicles away at full steam, Opal leading, down the center aisle of the dining hall.

"Fay," said Essie to her remaining breakfast companion, "I guess that just leaves the two of us!"

"Bacon!" shouted Fay, noticing that she had devoured her slice.

"I always love these morning conversations we have, Fay," added Essie, patting Fay's hand warmly.

Fay smiled at no one in particular.

Essie gestured to Santos who was passing by with a coffee pot to refill her cup.  She leaned back in her chair and glanced around the room.  Most of the residents of Happy Haven had cleared out. Only a few diners remained and the wait staff were hurriedly clearing the tables.  She tried to imagine the room as it was last night during the Bingo game.  Almost everyone had been there. Most of the residents loved their once-a-week Bingo game and most wouldn't miss it unless they were seriously ill or incapacitated.  So, most of the residents had witnessed Bob Weiderley's collapse.  If there had been anything unusual about the event, Essie was sure that Bob's three table companions would be the ones to notice.

## Chapter Four

*"Wrinkles should merely indicate where smiles have been."*
—Mark Twain

Essie was just finishing brushing her teeth. She had completed several other morning constitutionals and now she stood before her sink in her small bathroom staring into her mirror. It was the same face she saw every morning, but she had to remind herself sometimes that it was really her. The woman in the mirror was old—really old—with white hair and lots of wrinkles. When Essie thought of herself as Essie Cobb, she typically thought of herself as she used to be. As Essie Cobb, wife of John Cobb, banker. Or Essie Cobb, gardener.

She never ceased to be amazed at herself for finding a new career after her husband's death. Here she had spent her entire life as a wife and mother—noted only for her beautiful gardens. Then after John's death she had taken a part time job with Campbell's Nursery, the largest greenhouse in Reardon—not because she needed the money. She didn't. But because Edgar Campbell had cajoled her into joining his business as a consultant. She had spent many wonderful years working at Campbell's, helping customers solve their gardening problems. If there was a flower that wouldn't bloom or a tree that was having trouble sprouting, Essie was called in. After all, she had made her own home bloom, so why not help others do the same?

She realized as she looked in the mirror that her wrinkled, leathery skin was only partially due to old age. Much of it was from the hours and hours she had spent on her hands and knees in her garden and in the gardens of clients at Campbell's Nursery. Probably all the skin cream in the world wouldn't help her skin, but she didn't care because she had earned every wrinkle on her face and she was proud of them.   Oh, well!   She did have a beautiful head of white curls. *Enough reverie*, Essie, she said to herself.  She put the cap back on her tube of toothpaste.

She decided to take a walk around the Happy Haven complex. After all, she reasoned, a little exercise wouldn't hurt her.   Zipping down her hallway with her walker, she began her walk towards the main lobby.  Happy Haven's main foyer was divided in two parts. On entering, visitors found themselves in a large room with the main desk immediately on the right.  The foyer had a high ceiling and a beautiful brick fireplace centrally located.  Comfortable sofas and chairs were placed strategically around the fireplace area.  To the left was the entrance to the dining hall, scene of the Bingo collapse of Bob Weiderley.   To the right upon entrance was a cozier family-type room complete with sofas, chairs, and several television sets.  Beyond that, a small beauty shop, a mail room, and a chapel.   An elevator located between the foyer and the family room took residents and guests to the second floor.  On the second floor a recreational center and a small gym could be found.  The residents' rooms were located off various side hallways on both the first and second floors.

Essie's room was on the first floor, almost immediately off the family room to the right.   Marjorie's room was also on the first floor but on the other side of the family room.  Fay and Opal were both on the second floor.  Essie wasn't exactly certain where Bob Weiderley's room was, but she was certain that his tablemates would know.  She was now on the lookout for all of them—or at least one of them.  Some residents stayed in their rooms most of the time except for meals.   Others liked companionship and avoided their rooms except to sleep.  Essie hoped that Bob's tablemates were of this latter variety.

Essie wheeled her little red and black walker expertly into the family room, keeping an eye open for Rose, Hazel, or Evelyn. Several residents were seated in front of a large-screen television set, watching a news program.  Essie scooted her walker slowly around the viewing area, glancing, she hoped, surreptitiously, to see if any of Bob's three tablemates were there among the TV viewers. She regretted to note that none of the three appeared to be early morning news junkies. She continued on her expedition through the main foyer and past the fireplace. Several people were seated here. One old man was close to the fireplace, which was aglow with a warm blaze, even though it was technically spring. He was reading a newspaper. A woman was in a chair across from him. She appeared to be waiting for someone—probably a relative. No sign of Rose, Hazel, or Evelyn. Essie continued toward the dining hall. She could see through the glass wall that separated the dining hall from the rest of the complex. In the dining hall, the kitchen workers were busily preparing for the noontime meal. Several residents were seated at a table in the dining hall near the entrance, drinking coffee and chatting. They were ignored by the wait staff. Essie moved closer to the dining hall entrance, intent on checking the faces of the people at the table. Again, none of the group members appeared to be the three companions of Bob.

Moving away from the dining hall, Essie decided to stop at the mail boxes, located directly across from the dining hall entrance on a wall that separated it from the foyer. Leaning on her walker, she bent over to the lowest row and peeked into box number C103, the same as her room number. As usual, her box was empty. She seldom received any mail. Sometimes, Happy Haven put flyers in the mail boxes to announce various activities, but no such flyer was there today. Essie rose with difficulty from her kneeling position to find herself facing one of the three people for whom she was searching.

"Hazel," she exclaimed, tentatively. "Are you Hazel Brubaker?"

"Yes," responded the tall woman, bent precariously over her walker, as she had also been checking her mailbox. Essie was resigned to using her walker because of the osteoarthritis in her back, but she reveled in the fact that she could move it with relative speed. Hazel Brubaker seemed to be having trouble merely making the walker move forward a few inches. "I'm Hazel."

"You share a table with Bob Weiderley, don't you?" Essie asked.

"Yes," replied Hazel Brubaker. "Yes. I do." Her hands shook almost imperceptibly and her lower lip started to tremble.

"I'm so sorry about Bob," continued Essie in a soft voice, moving closer to Hazel. "He's such a friendly person. I played canasta with him several times."

"Yes," agreed Hazel, obviously struggling to control her shaking hands by gripping the handles of her walker to the point where Essie noted her knuckles were becoming white.

"Have you heard how he's doing?"

"He's at Fairview," responded Hazel. "He's in a coma." She looked down at her hands.

"Yes," said Essie, placing a hand on the woman's clenched fingers. "I had heard. Do they know what happened?"

"I don't know," said Hazel, still staring at her hands. "I don't know. I wish I knew what happened."

"Me too," agreed Essie. "I always thought Bob was so athletic—so healthy."

"He is. I mean, I thought he was."

"Have you spoken to anyone? Does anyone know how he's doing?" asked Essie, continuing to press the woman's hand.

"Rose is supposed to go see him today. Her daughter promised to take her."

"That's nice," said Essie, smiling. "Rose is part of your table, right?"

"Yes," said Hazel. "She was—is—close to Bob."

"Oh, I see." Essie didn't see, but Hazel said this last as if Essie should know. "Do you think she's at the hospital now?"

"I don't know," responded Hazel, and then with a blank look, she guided her walker around and started moving away.

"Goodbye, Hazel," called out Essie. "My best wishes for Bob's speedy recovery."

Hazel continued pushing her walker slowly through the main foyer and into the family room where she disappeared from Essie's sight.

*How strange*, thought Essie. *That woman seemed terribly upset, but she didn't seem to know very much about Bob Weiderley. One would think that she'd want to talk about someone whom she seemed to care about that much.* She had acquired one clue, however. Rose was evidently close to Bob—and she was probably at this very moment visiting him in the hospital. Now, Essie simply needed to determine when Rose would be returning and ambush her—that is, wait for her return.

"Essie, what are you doing out here by the mailboxes? Are you planning to accost the mailman?"

Essie turned abruptly to discover Sue Barber, the Social Director standing behind her.

"Good morning, Miss Barber," she greeted the attractive young woman. "I was checking my mailbox."

"You're a bit early, you know," noted Sue. "Or, you're quite late!"

Essie laughed with the attractive blonde. She liked Sue Barber, not only for her sense of humor which she brought to bear in many of the activities she planned for the residents, but also in her casual, friendly manner. "Ted usually gets here around one o'clock!"

"I know, Miss Barber," said Essie. "I just thought you might have put a flyer in the boxes about that upcoming trip to the botanical gardens." *Nice save, Essie*, she thought to herself.

"Oh, the botanical gardens!" exclaimed Sue. "Now I remember! You're the gardener. I believe one of your tablemates told me you're some sort of plant expert."

"I have grown a flower or two in my day," agreed Essie, modestly.

"Then you'll love the botanical gardens," gushed Sue. "You should sign up for the field trip next week! It will be a blast!"

"I'm sure it will be," said Essie, "A blast! I'll just go do that right now, Miss Barber." She gave her walker a circular push and pivoted around the social director, heading off in the direction of the main desk where she knew she would find the sign-up sheet for the field trip to the botanical gardens, which she would absolutely not sign. She avoided field trips because they made her feel claustrophobic and she liked the freedom to move around where she wanted when she wanted. Like right now.

As she reached the main desk, she glanced over her shoulder to see Sue Barber continuing to smile sweetly in her direction. Essie stopped at the main desk and grabbed a pencil and a clipboard. Glancing at the top of the clipboard, she saw the heading which said "Free Colonoscopies." Quickly she faked signing her name on the sign-up sheet with a flourish. Then glancing towards Sue Barber at the mailboxes, she returned her sweet smile and headed off through the family room towards the elevator.

As she rode the elevator to the second floor, she contemplated the reaction she had gleaned from Hazel Brubaker. She'd seemed very upset which could be merely because she *was* very upset. Her tablemate was seriously ill—in a coma. She imagined she would be very upset if Opal or Marjorie or Fay were hospitalized, particularly if one of them were in a coma. It probably wasn't unusual that Hazel Brubaker was as upset as she seemed, Essie reasoned. She had discovered that another of Bob's tablemates—Rose Lane—was actually visiting him at the hospital. She was certain she would recognize Rose, probably in the company of her daughter—when she returned from the hospital. All she had to do was wait somewhere inconspicuous where she could observe people entering the main door and then she would accost this Rose Lane and ask her about Bob and his condition.

When she arrived at the second floor, she rolled her walker to a comfy sofa that rimmed the railing around the second floor lobby. From this position, she would be able to see Rose Lane when she returned from the hospital. Of course, Essie realized, once she saw her, it would take her a while to get back down to the first floor on the elevator again. Rose might get to her room before Essie had a chance to talk to her. Oh, well. It was just a chance she'd have to take. If she remained downstairs, Sue Barber was liable to chat her up again about the botanical gardens field trip—especially when she discovered that Essie had not actually signed up for the trip as she promised. Essie placed her walker at the edge of the sofa and slid herself down into the soft cushions of the couch. This sofa was endlessly better than the thinly padded rubber seat on her walker where she typically sat when she had to wait for long periods of time. She could even fall asleep here—just like Fay did. Oh, my. *Contain yourself, Essie*, she thought. *Pay attention and watch for Rose's entrance.*

As she focused her eagle eyes on the main entrance doors, numerous people entered and exited. Some were residents or their relatives. Some were delivery men. Some medical support people or staff of Happy Haven and various others. Eventually, a short woman with short bluish gray locks and a voluminous bosom entered, leaning on a carved mahogany cane, helped along by a younger blonde woman who looked almost like her double, with a short pixie-cut haircut. Rose Lane. And daughter.

Essie clutched the handle of her walker and extracted herself from the sofa with great difficulty. Quickly as she could, she headed to the elevator and pressed the button. The machine arrived almost instantly and she entered the compartment and rode down to the first floor. As she exited the elevator on the ground level, she rolled as fast as she could through the foyer, looking for Rose Lane and her daughter. She glimpsed them heading down the first floor side hallway between the mailboxes and the dining hall. She zipped towards them.

"Rose!" she called out. "Rose!" The lady turned at the sound of her name, along with her daughter. Essie moved toward the mother-daughter couple. "Rose, hello. I'm Essie Cobb. I was speaking to Hazel and she suggested I talk to you."

"Oh, my!" said Rose, smiling at her daughter and then looking back to Essie. "Hello, Essie. I know you. This is my daughter Dora." There were greetings all around.

"I understand you've been visiting Bob," said Essie.

"Yes," confirmed Rose. "We just returned."

"How is he doing? We're all so concerned about him."

"I know," said Rose. "Everyone here is worried. Bob is a favorite here."

"Such a sweet man," interjected Dora, the daughter.

"He's still in a coma, but the doctors are hopeful."

"They think he'll recover?"

"I hope so. Although they did say that the longer he remains in the coma the worse things look." She glanced quickly at her daughter. A tear rolled down her cheek. "I'm sorry. I sat with him and held his hand. I tried to cheer him up but I don't know if he heard me or not."

"I just don't understand why he collapsed in the first place," said Essie. "I always thought of Bob as a really sturdy fellow. You know, so athletic. He was always doing aerobic exercises."

"I know," agreed Rose. "He did sit-ups and push-ups regularly. He prided himself on taking really good care of himself."

"Maybe it was stress," offered Essie.

"Stress?" said Rose, her small nose twitching as she glanced again at her daughter.

"I mean, maybe something was bothering him. Sometimes, they say that stress can be just as dangerous as high cholesterol or lack of activity in causing heart attacks. . ."

"Oh, it wasn't a heart attack," noted Rose. "The doctors aren't certain exactly what it was—or is—but Bob's nurse said quite specifically that it's not a heart attack—or a stroke."

"But it could be stress?"

"I guess," responded Rose. "I guess it could be anything else. Who knows?"

"Had Bob discussed anything with you that was bothering him?"

"No . . ."

"Nothing?"

"Nothing he said," said Rose, again looking towards her daughter.

"I sense a but," offered Essie, glancing from one woman to another, sensing their discomfort.

"It's funny, Essie. I was just telling my daughter. Bob did seem agitated at dinner."

"At dinner?"

"Yes, last night. He was just fine at lunch—the regular old Bob—cheerful, friendly, outgoing. Then, at dinner, he was quiet. He seemed nervous, like something was bothering him."

"Do you know what that something was?"

"No. I don't have a clue. But I'm guessing that whatever it was, it was what led to his collapse during Bingo. You could ask Evelyn."

"Evelyn?"

"Yes, our other tablemate. She might know. Sometimes, I think—I'm not sure—but sometimes Bob stayed after dinner. They talked. Evelyn is a very good listener."

"Mom," whispered Rose Lane's daughter.

"I need to get going, Essie. If you want to talk to Evelyn, you can probably find her in the chapel around this time."

"I wouldn't want to disturb her."

Rose beamed from ear to ear. "You wouldn't disturb Evelyn. I promise." She clutched Essie's arm, then turned abruptly and transferred her weight to her daughter's arm and the two walked slowly into the residents' hallway.

Essie lost no time pushing her walker swiftly through the foyer and family room. Down the back entrance to the family room ran a narrow hallway that led to a small room which had been turned into a non-denominational chapel. As she guided her walker through the doorway, she noted one woman kneeling near the front altar. She assumed it was Evelyn Cudahy because the woman was wearing a bright flowered scarf wrapped around her head. Essie moved between the pews and up the central aisle of the chapel as quietly as possible. She seated herself behind and across from the kneeling woman.

Soon, the woman must have realized that someone else was in the small chapel, because she turned her head. When she saw Essie, she smiled and rose. Walking towards her, Essie was impressed with how her face seemed to glow—surprising for someone undergoing chemotherapy, she thought.

"Essie Cobb," said the scarved woman.

"Evelyn Cudahy?" asked Essie.

"Yes," she replied. "Are you looking for me?"

"I hate to intrude."

"It's fine. If you want to talk to me, we can talk here. No one else is around. If someone comes in, though, we'll have to leave."

"I understand."

"You're concerned about Bob," said Evelyn as she sat beside Essie in the pew.

"How did you know?"

"I'm concerned about him too!"

"Oh," said Essie, stammering, "I thought. . . I thought. . ."

"You thought I was here praying for myself?"

"I . . . I . . ."

"There's nothing wrong with praying for yourself and—believe me—I do my share of it. But today, my prayers are primarily for Bob."

"Rose Lane suggested I talk to you. She thought you might know what was bothering him."

"I wish I did. Maybe I could have helped him. He has certainly helped me."

"He has?"

"I mean, he was—is—a good . . . friend. He's always there for me. He talks to me. He lets me talk to him. If I knew anything I could do or say to help him I surely would."

"It sounds like the two of you have a very special relationship."

"Yes. We do. I guess possibly because neither of us has any other family."

"No family at all?"

"No. I never married and I was an only child. The same for Bob. We feel quite a kinship. Most everyone else here at Happy Haven has children—or at least nephews or nieces."

"I can see how that might be," answered Essie. She remained quiet, admiring the strong-minded and capable woman before her. Finally she spoke. "Rose suggested that Bob seemed particularly agitated at dinner last night."

"Yes, he did." She looked down, her forehead suddenly becoming a mass of wrinkles on her previously smooth face.

"Even more so at Bingo. He even told me he needed to talk to me after Bingo. Not wanted to talk to me, but needed to talk to me. I'm guessing that whatever was bothering him was eating away at him so much that he felt the need to unburden himself to me."

"And he'd done that before?"

"Yes, but, Essie, the things that typically bothered Bob were the things you would imagine. He was so lonely when he first came here—I guess—six years ago. Even so, he always tried to be cheerful. Happy Haven really became his family. Being here was probably the first time in his life that he finally felt as if he had a family. I can't imagine what could have been bothering him last night, but it wasn't just his typical loneliness."

"Rose said he was fine at lunch but at supper he seemed upset."

"That's what I noticed too. Rose and I both did. Hazel too. It was very strange. I really expected to get some answers after Bingo, but then Bob collapsed and now I don't know if we'll ever know."

"Rose visited him today at the hospital," offered Essie.

"I know," answered Evelyn. Then she said, "I so wish I could be there for him, but they won't let me go anywhere near the hospital, particularly to any patient floors while I'm undergoing chemo. I really want to be there for him. This is like a substitute," she said, indicating the chapel with her hand.

"And you can't guess at what might have been bothering him?"

"I wish I knew," said Evelyn, "but I just don't. Whatever it was, though, it was something that came up suddenly. Because I know for certain that it wasn't bothering him at all at lunch and by supper it was consuming him."

"It's too bad he didn't confide in you at supper. Maybe there would be something we—you—some of us could have done to help him."

"That's what I keep wondering," she sighed. "But it's too late for fretting over that now. We just need to concentrate now on helping him to recover and come out of this coma."

"I agree, Evelyn." Essie grasped the woman's hands in hers and squeezed them. "I'm going to leave you now so you can continue your efforts on Bob's behalf."

"Thank you, Essie, for your concern about Bob. I mean, you hardly knew him."

"He's one of us, Evelyn. As you said yourself, we're all a family at Happy Haven." She smiled as she stood up. Then grabbing the handles of her walker, she maneuvered the device around and headed out of the chapel and down the back hallway towards the family room.

# Chapter Five

*"Age is a high price to pay for maturity."*
—Tom Stoppard

As she rolled back down her hallway towards her apartment, she saw in the distance a man standing at her doorway, knocking. *Who is that?* she wondered. As she got closer, she realized that the young man (he was probably fifty-something, but when you're over ninety as Essie was, someone in their fifties is young) was Darrell McKinney, her financial advisor. *Oh, great!* she thought. *Just what I don't need now.* Darrell was a superb advisor and had done a spectacular job maintaining her portfolio and seeing to it that she didn't go broke (as she phrased it—Darrell phrased it as "maximizing her assets and minimizing her liabilities"). Unfortunately, he pestered her. Every time she turned around, he was calling her or at her door wanting to make what she perceived as a miniscule change in her finances. She'd tried to tell him to do what he thought best. She'd tried to give him "carte blanche" but Darrell didn't seem to get the message. He was determined to "advise" her just as he had "advised" her husband John for many years before his death. And feeling sorry for the man (after all, Darrell probably missed John as much as she did), she continued to foster their relationship.

"Darrell," she called out. "Visiting again? So soon? Seems like you were just here the other day." She smiled sweetly.

"Essie," responded Darrell, briefcase in hand. "I dropped by to check on you and to go over a few changes I think we might like to make in your portfolio." Essie opened her door (she never locked it unless she was actually leaving the facility which was hardly ever) and Darrell followed her into her small living room.

Essie rolled over to her favorite chair and plopped down, leaving her walker beside her.  Darrell followed and took a position on the love seat directly across from her.  He opened his case and brought out several folders and papers.  Immediately he began talking about the various changes he wanted to make in Essie's stock holdings.

To Essie, it sounded like, "waa, waa, waa.  And then we could blah, blah, blah.  On the other hand, we might duh, duh, duh."  She recalled how much her late husband had enjoyed playing the stock market and the times he and the then young Darrell had spent together at their kitchen table plotting their moves.  Over the years, John's efforts along with Darrell's input had made Essie a comfortably well-to-do woman.  She was certainly grateful for their efforts, but she didn't share John's intense fascination with the stock market.  And she never was able to convey this message to Darrell.  She just listened to him every time he brought her a new idea and hoped that her husband's faith in the man had not been and would not be misplaced.

"And just how is my portfolio doing, Darrell?" she asked when Darrell stopped for air midway through his spiel.

"Magnificently, Essie!" replied Darrell, his warm brown eyes twinkling.  "John knew what he was doing when he set up this portfolio for you.  For example, we have this Cracked Liberty Bell Fund.  Now you've had over 500 shares of CLBF for going on six years.  My recommendation is to move at least half of that over to Mutual Imagine Longtime Investments.  They're a new company and their rate of return has tripled in just the last six months.  This is something I think we want to get in on."

"It sure sounds like something we should get in on.  Lots of numbers there, Darrell.  Very impressive."

"And, Essie.  Your LSD Bond Fund—the one we doubled last year.  It really took off last month.  Defied the market and the other market indicators.  You know, I typically advise against bonds, but those bond funds can't be beat.  I'd recommend we add to our holdings with LSD and decrease our holdings in some fund that isn't producing as well—say, maybe, the Tread Gently Exchange Traded Fund."

"I'm all for LSD.  I missed out on it back in the sixties."

"I'm also going to recommend we put in place a stop-order at $5000 for all of our prime holdings.  That means you'll receive a notification when a fund reaches that level and we'll have to decide whether or not we want to continue holding that particular fund above that level.  If that happens, I'll call you . . ."

"How about I just give you permission right now to do what you think is best?  If that happens," she suggested coyly.

"All right," said Darrell slowly, peering at her, his long thick eyelashes totally wasted, she often thought, on a man so completely obsessed with money.  "If that's what you want to do, but I have no problem consulting with you about each of these decisions."

"I know, Darrell," she said, "and truly I appreciate it, but I trust you.  I really do.  I trust that you'll do what's best for my money— and for me!"

"Okay, Essie," he agreed.  "But you should know that I would never do anything to damage your trust in me.  I consider the time I spent working with your husband, a wonderful period for me. John trusted me and helped me get established and I promised him I would take good care of you and I intend to do just that."

"I know," she responded.  "Not all women are as lucky as I am. There are certainly many women right here in Happy Haven who struggle financially.  I guess their husbands didn't plan the way John did."

"Believe me, Essie.  I hear about them.  I do.  Actually, I have several clients who are residents here at Happy Haven.  I try to get around to all of them when I visit.  But visiting you is far and away the easiest of my duties because I always have good news for you. Not so for some of my other clients who started investing too late or made foolish decisions."

"I didn't know you had other clients here, Darrell."

"Yes, indeed.  Actually, the main reason I'm here today is because of what happened to one of them.  I just dropped by to see you as an afterthought.  You may know him—Bob Weiderley."

"Bob?  You're Bob's financial advisor?"

"I am.  You know Bob?"

"I don't know him well, but I was there last night when he collapsed."

"Oh, dear.  How awful for you!"

"Darrell, is Bob having financial difficulties?  I know.  I know. I have no business asking, but he was obviously in terrible distress last night when he collapsed at Bingo.  Several of us were wondering what he was upset about.  I was thinking if he'd lost a lot of money recently and that's why you were coming over, maybe that's what upset him . . ."

"Oh, no! No, Essie!  It can't be that.  If Bob is—was—upset— it's not about his finances.  Actually, I shouldn't say this.  I have no business telling you this, but I can't imagine Bob would object to your knowing, particularly as you're so worried about him.  But truthfully, Essie, Bob is not hurting financially.  Not at all."

"Oh?  I'd never heard him talk about his career or anything so I didn't know his situation."

"Bob, I believe I can safely say, is—was—quite an inventor when he was younger and he secured patents on a number of very successful devices that are used in industry today.  Nothing you'd have heard of, but devices that make the manufacturing of various computer components easier.  Suffice it to say, Essie, Bob Weiderley is a very wealthy man."

"He is?"

"Absolutely."

"His tablemates claim he was horribly upset last night and they don't know why . . ."

"It wasn't because he'd lost any money or was in any financial trouble of any sort.  That's for sure."

Essie sat in her chair trying to reconcile this new, amazing information with the reality of Bob's hospitalization.

"I wonder what could have upset him so?"

"Not everything bad is related to money, Essie," noted Darrell. Strange, thought Essie, that Darrell would make this observation seeing as how Darrell didn't think about anything but money.

"He didn't have any family," she added.

"True," agreed Darrell. "Sad, of course, but it certainly simplified his will. Family members often cause problems for rich people when they try to plan their wills."

"You know about his will?" she asked carefully.

"He did discuss it with me from time to time. I am his financial advisor. Of course, I'm not his attorney, but as his financial advisor, he wanted me to be aware of where his money would go in the event of his death."

"And where would it go?" asked Essie cautiously.

"You don't know?" laughed Darrell. "I thought surely he would have told you all."

"What do you mean, Darrell?"

"He left it to Happy Haven. All of it. All five million dollars of it. He left it here! To the Happy Haven Assisted Living Facility."

# Chapter Six

*"I still have a full deck; I just shuffle slower now."*
—Author Unknown

"Essie," said Marjorie, poking her friend. "It's your turn. Play."

"Um, I'll meld," responded Essie, glancing down at her cards and then placing most of them in columns in front of her. She and her tablemates had gathered in the family room for a quick game of canasta before lunch call. They were lucky to get through a round in an hour because Fay constantly had to be awakened to play her hand. Despite this delay, Fay usually made relatively competent moves. Her sleepiness was apparently more an issue of exhaustion or boredom rather than an indication of senility.

Opal followed Essie by adding a king of hearts to one of her columns.

Marjorie poked Fay who sat on her left. Fay awoke promptly, took a quick glance at the previously played cards, her own hand, and discarded a black three of clubs. Marjorie also played a black three.

"Essie, back to you!" chortled Opal to Essie who was staring out the full-length glass window.

"Essie," added Marjorie, "get with the game!"

"What?" said Essie, looking from one friend to another.

"Are you still fretting over Bob Weiderley?" asked Marjorie.

"You didn't go pester his tablemates, did you?" asked Opal.

"I didn't pester anyone, Opal," said Essie, defensively. "I merely spoke with them. And, they don't know why Bob collapsed."

"I told you so," said Opal. "Your snooping is just a waste of time."

"Actually, it wasn't," said Essie. "I found out from Evelyn that Bob had become very upset yesterday about something, sometime between lunch and dinner. He said he wanted to talk to her about it after Bingo, but of course, we know what happened there."

"Does she know what it was about?" asked Marjorie.

"No, unfortunately not," said Essie, playing another card.

"Then it's just like I said. None of them really knows anything."

"But they know that he was unusually upset about something very specific."

"What could it be, Essie?" asked Marjorie. "What could it possibly be?"

Essie set her hand of cards face down on the table and leaned in close to her three friends. Fay woke up and, startled to see three faces bent so close together, joined them.

"I know one thing it isn't," she whispered to the three women.

"What?" they all asked in unison.

"Money."

"Why do you say that?" asked Marjorie.

"Because I found out just a little while ago that Bob Weiderley is not hurting for money. Indeed, he's not hurting at all. He's actually a multi-millionaire."

"What?" asked Opal.

"Don't ask me how I know, but I know. And that's not the half of it. Guess who's the beneficiary in his will?"

"I don't know," said Marjorie. "He doesn't have any family— no children."

"Right," agreed Essie. "Bob has left his entire estate to us!"

"Us?" replied Opal, aghast. "You mean the four of us?"

"No, silly! Us! Happy Haven! His entire estate goes to Happy Haven!"

"Who knows this?" asked Marjorie.

"I'm assuming Happy Haven knows. That means Violet."

"Violet!" shouted Fay out loud. "Violet knows!"

"Quiet, Fay!" shushed Essie.

"Essie," said Marjorie, her index finger pointing in the air. "Does that mean that you suspect Violet of—of causing Bob's collapse at Bingo last night?"

Essie looked back and forth at the three faces. The three women stared at her with great anticipation. She hesitated before she spoke.

"I don't think so," she replied carefully. "I mean, Violet doesn't own Happy Haven; she's just the Director. If Happy Haven gets a lot of money from someone's inheritance—and I'm sure it does from time to time—Violet doesn't profit personally."

"She did get new curtains in her office last year," noted Opal slyly, a satisfied smirk on her face.

"New curtains!" said Fay, nodding.

"But not five million dollar curtains," added Essie is a conspiratorial whisper.

"So, who does profit if Happy Haven is left money in a will? What do they do with it? Does any person benefit?" This was Marjorie thinking out loud. The other women listened and nodded as she made each point.

"There's a Board of Directors," said Essie. "HH is run by a company which has a Board. I don't believe it's owned by an individual. I've never paid much attention. My children pay all my bills."

"The Board probably just put it in their endowment and use it to pay their taxes," noted Opal.

"Oh, you would know from endowments, Opal?" sassed Marjorie.

"Ladies," cautioned Essie. "This is all speculation. Remember, Bob is—as far as we know—still very much alive."

"Very much alive!" agreed Fay, nodding so hard her glasses fell off of her nose.

"Yes, but five million dollars seems like quite a motive to me!" suggested Marjorie.

"It's only a motive if you are the beneficiary—and you're not—and neither is Violet!" Opal argued.

"What I recommend we do is keep our eyes and ears open!" said Essie. "And don't let on we know anything about Bob's finances or his will."

"I won't tell a soul," said Marjorie.

"Neither will I," said Opal. "Not that you need to ask."

"Tell who what?" asked Fay.

"Never mind, Fay," said Essie, patting Fay's hand. "You just keep doing what you're doing." Fay smiled, picked up her cards, and peered at them intently.

"Canasta!" shouted Fay and placed the remaining cards in her hand on the columns on the board.

"She just won!" said Opal, aghast. "I didn't even think she was paying attention."

"You sly minx, Fay," said Marjorie, pinching one of Fay's chubby cheeks.

"It just goes to show that you should never underestimate little old ladies in wheel chairs. You never know what they might be up to!" said Essie with a smile.

"Good morning, residents!" rang out a soothing voice over the intercom system. The four friends silenced their discussion and returned to their card game, as the melodious voice read announcements for the next day, including a list of upcoming social activities.

"And don't forget to sign up for the botanical gardens field trip," urged the voice. "Remember, the Reardon local gardens have some of the most exquisite indigenous flowering plants in the four-state area. We still have room for three more participants. Just add your name to the sign-up sheet at the front desk. Buses leave for the gardens this Thursday."

"You should go on that trip," suggested Marjorie to Essie. "You love gardening!"

"Not someone else's gardening!" responded Essie. "I hate field trips."

"Why on earth would you say that?" queried Opal.

"I hate being cooped up."

"Cooped up?" asked Marjorie. "You mean cooped up away from a bathroom?"

"That too," noted Essie. "There's never a toilet around when you need one."

"Toilet!" added Fay, as she played another card, reaching her pudgy arm out and plopping the queen down on her column.

"Some of those big buses have toilets," suggested Opal. "But probably not the Happy Haven bus."

"I would never use a toilet on a bus!" exclaimed Essie. "What do you take me for? A homeless person? There's probably graffiti on the walls. Besides, the problem is getting to the bathroom on the bus—in time."

"Oh, I see," offered Opal sympathetically.

"Essie," scowled Marjorie. "You shouldn't let a little—incontinence—get in your way. I know I don't! They make some remarkable products for women like us nowadays." Marjorie smoothed her skirt and sat up a little taller in her chair.

"Then you have no shame, Marjorie!" countered Essie.

The announcer's voice continued over the intercom. "Happy Haven will be sending flowers to the following residents who are hospitalized: Glenda Stearns, Mamie Morgan, Eloise Steinberger, and Bob Weiderley. If you would like to sign a get well card for any of these residents, see Phyllis at the front desk. You have until 7 p.m. tonight."

"I guess if they're sending Bob flowers and a get well card, it must mean he's still alive," said Opal. She bit her lip, contemplating her next move.

"But is he still in a coma? That's the more important question," added Essie. She looked at Opal, waiting for her to make her move. Finally, Opal discarded a six of diamonds.

"Fay, it's your turn!" said Marjorie, nudging the little woman to her left. Fay shook herself and looked pointedly at the cards on the table and squinted her eyes. Then, with a slow, careful movement she placed all of the cards in her hand on the columns of cards on the table in front of her.

"I'm out," she said, smiling sweetly at her three card partners.

"What!" screamed Opal. "You can't be out! We barely started!"

"How did you do that, Fay?" asked Marjorie, bending over and examining Fay's cards.

"I don't believe it," said Essie, shaking her head. "No, I take that back. Actually, now, I'll believe anything."

"Oh, well," said Marjorie in resignation as she stood up. "It's almost time for lunch. I need to get to my room for a bit. I'll see you all in a while." She gathered her purse, placed it atop her walker seat, and wheeled herself away.

Opal gathered the cards from the table and placed them in a box and then wheeled over and returned them to a cupboard near the wall.

"Fay," said Essie. "What do you think happened to Bob Weiderley? I think you know more than you let on." She leaned in towards the rosy-cheeked woman with the thin but fluffy head of grey hair and waited for what she assumed would be a revelatory remark.

"Box," said Fay. Essie turned around towards Opal who was placing the box of cards in the cupboard.

"The card box?" she asked Fay. "The box where we keep the cards? Is that what you mean?"

"Box," replied Fay enigmatically. Opal wheeled back to the table and remained standing.

"Fay, are you ready to go back to your room? I have some things to do before lunch. We'll see you at lunch, Essie." Opal headed towards the elevator with Fay following behind in her wheelchair. The two soon disappeared behind the elevator doors. Essie sat at the card table, thinking. Then, she pulled herself up and rolled her walker away the short distance down her hallway to her apartment.

## Chapter Seven

*"A man is not old as long as he is seeking something."*
—Jean Rostand

At lunch, the four women continued their furtive discussion about Bob Weiderley and the cause of his sudden collapse. Essie noticed immediately as she looked around the room that all three of Bob's tablemates were at their assigned dining spots. She smiled and waved discreetly at them from across the dining hall. Santos arrived and the women placed their orders—with the most popular request being Croque Monsieur.

"Let's put our heads together," said Essie as soon as Santos had returned to the kitchen. "We need to consider everything we now know about Bob and his situation. Then we need to decide what we need to do next."

"Do?" exclaimed Opal. "What can we possibly do, Essie? We're four old ladies in an assisted living facility."

"I don't know—maybe nothing," said Essie, ignoring Opal. "But let's not get ahead of ourselves. First, let's figure out exactly what we do know."

"We know that Bob collapsed during Bingo and had to be taken away in an ambulance. We know he's in a coma in Fairview Hospital now," said Marjorie.

"We know that Bob was really upset about something," said Opal.

"And we know that whatever upset him, happened sometime yesterday between lunch and dinner," added Essie.

"We know that Bob is a multi-millionaire," said Opal, lowering her voice to a whisper, "and that he's left his entire fortune to Happy Haven."

"We also know that Bob has no family," said Marjorie.

"That anyone knows about," said Essie.

"So," said Essie, "we can conclude—if nothing else—that it is possible that someone might have had a motive to murder Bob."

"But who? Does it mean that everyone who lives at Happy Haven has a motive to kill him because he's willed his money to Happy Haven?" asked Marjorie.

"Unlikely," said Essie. "But I don't think we know enough about Happy Haven—its structure, its hierarchy to make a determination about that."

"How can we find out?" asked Marjorie, bouncing a bit in her chair with excitement.

"Let me think about that," replied Essie, just as Santos arrived with their Croque Monsieurs. The women ceased their discussion and for a few moments all four heads were bent over the crispy, crunchy sandwiches filled with ham and cheese. Soon, all four plates were nothing but a landscape of crumbs. The four friends sipped their coffees and teas as Santos placed chocolate pudding cake before each.

"Ladies like Croque Monsieurs?" asked Santos as he distributed the desserts.

"Oh, yes, Santos," said Marjorie. "Delicious! I wish we had them more often."

"They're tasty," agreed Opal, "but I'm afraid they're quite fattening."

"Ladies at this table no need worry fattening," said Santos, cheerfully.

"You're a diplomat, Santos," added Essie. "Do you hear anything from Bob Weiderley's table? I see his tablemates are here."

"Yes," said Santos, wiping his hands on his dish towel. "Mr. Bob's ladies say he still in coma. But say doctors very hopeful."

"Yes, that's what we heard," noted Essie. "I just wish we knew more. Santos, you waited on Bob last night at dinner, didn't you?"

"Yes, Miss Essie. Mr. Bob very worried."

"You noticed it too?"

"Ladies look at him a lot. Ladies very worried for Mr. Bob."

"What did Bob eat last night?"

"Can't remember," replied the waiter. "Oh, yes, now remember. Mr. Bob not very hungry, he said. He only wanted some soup. I bring him chicken soup. He only eat a little bit of it. You ladies want more coffee?" he asked finally.

"No," replied Essie, "I'm fine."

"Me too," added Marjorie.

"Same here," said Opal.

"Coffee, Miss Fay?" Santos asked the wheelchair-bound lady, leaning in and speaking in her ear as she was snoring softly.

"What?" asked Fay, startled to discover the young brown face directly in front of hers.

Santos pulled back a bit, and repeated his request, "Would you like some more coffee, Miss Fay?"

Fay shook her head, smiling warmly at the waiter. Her cheeks reddened—even more than her usual rosy glow. Santos shrugged and headed back to the kitchen.

Essie glanced at Opal and Marjorie with a double-take.

"Fay?" asked Essie. "I think you like Santos, don't you?"

"Who?" answered Fay, turning away from Essie. She quickly dozed off again.

"Why did you ask him about what Bob ate for supper?" asked Opal.

"I was just wondering if it might have been possible for someone to poison his meal?" she said.

"What?" exclaimed Marjorie, dropping her half-filled cup and splattering coffee on her lap.

"I said I was thinking that it might have been possible that Bob was poisoned," repeated Essie.

"Why would anyone want to poison him?" asked Opal, also plunking her cup down on her saucer.

"Doesn't anyone remember that five million dollar will?" Essie whispered.

"But no one at his table would benefit personally from his will," said Marjorie.

"It wouldn't have to be someone at his table," contemplated Essie, still holding her cup and bringing it to her lips for a brief sip.

"Who are you thinking?" asked Opal.

"Just think. Bob's table is right by the door. People are walking by it as they go in and out. All sorts of people come and go that way—possibly people no one knows—and anyone could slip some powder or liquid into Bob's soup without him or any of his tablemates noticing." Essie had set forth her case. Now she sat back in her chair and waited for her jury's reaction.

"That's ridiculous, Essie!" said Marjorie. "Surely, one of them would notice if somebody tried to put something in Bob's food."

"I agree!" said Opal. "Not to mention the fact that we haven't established that anyone had any reason to want Bob dead—except for the money in his will—which we all know wasn't left to any one person here, but to the entire facility. I don't see how that would be a motive for murder."

"And," added Marjorie, "he didn't collapse at supper; he collapsed at Bingo, and he wasn't eating then."

"It could have been a slow-acting poison!" argued Essie.

"If that's the case, maybe someone poisoned him three weeks ago when he was on the field trip to the natural history museum," suggested Opal.

"Really, Essie," exclaimed Marjorie, "you are usually so level-headed, but this line of reasoning is just. . . just foolish!"

"You're right," agreed Essie, looking directly at Marjorie. "I don't know why I didn't think of it . . ."

"Of what?" asked Marjorie.

"Bob wasn't poisoned in his soup . . ." she said. "He was poisoned some other way. Possibly he was so agitated because he'd had some sort of encounter with the poisoner. And it must have occurred yesterday afternoon."

"You are really off the deep end," said Opal, shaking her head.

"Oh, I don't know if he was poisoned, but something happened yesterday afternoon—between lunch and dinner—that upset him terribly. This something probably led to or at least contributed to his collapse. Are we agreed on that?"

The women nodded in agreement, even Fay, although Fay continued to nod after the others had stopped.

"Then we have to find out what it was," pronounced Essie.

"But, Essie, you said that none of the women at his table even had a clue about what was upsetting Bob. If they don't know, how do you expect us to find out?" pleaded Marjorie.

"I can think of one way," said Essie.

"What?" asked Marjorie and Opal. Fay looked from one friend to another.

"Break into his apartment."

"What?"

"Break into Bob's apartment," repeated Essie.

"Just what do you expect to find there?" asked Opal.

"I don't know. Maybe a clue as to who poisoned him or why he was so upset last night or something," she offered. Then she sighed and gave them all a sad smile.

"I don't think it's wise, Essie," said Marjorie. "You could get in lots of trouble."

"What are they going to do to me? Arrest me? Old lady breaks into old man's room at assisted living facility! Story at ten! All they'd do is give me a reprimand—like I'm a school girl," Essie explained.

"Actually," said Opal. "It probably wouldn't be hard at all. I mean, hardly anyone locks their doors unless they're leaving the building."

"True," agreed Marjorie.

"I say we head out to Bob's room right now and case the joint," said Essie, cajoling.

"Wait a minute," said Opal, holding up her hands as Marjorie and Essie started to leave. "Where is Bob's room?"

"Ooops!" said Essie, sitting back down. "I could ask Hazel or Rose or Evelyn but I'm afraid they'd want to know why we wanted to know where Bob's room was."

"True," agreed Marjorie. "I know he's on the second floor, but I don't know what wing he's in."

"We could just roam up and down all the residential hallways on the second floor looking at the names on the doors until we find it," suggested Essie.

"I should help Fay get back to her room," said Opal.

"Then Marjorie and I will go look for Bob's room," said Essie. "You take Fay back. It's probably better that we keep this a smaller group so none of the aides or directors get suspicious."

The four women nodded to each other and then headed out of the dining hall. Opal and Fay went first while Essie and Marjorie sat in the lobby for a few moments. After a while, they rose and pressed the button for the elevator. When they reached the second floor, they hesitated.

"Let's think about this first," said Essie. "We'd probably save time if each of us takes a different hallway. If you find Bob's room, you come find me. If I find his room, I'll come find you."

"All right, Essie," agreed Marjorie. "I'll take the two hallways on the right and you take the ones on the left." Essie agreed to this plan and the two women started to roll their walkers away down the first hallway they intended to check.

As Essie glided down the silent hallway, she realized how much quieter the second floor was compared to the first floor. She had gotten used to the ambient noise from the lobby and family room that seeped through her walls. Up here, the hallways were like a tomb—no people, no sound. Essie moved her walker along the carpeted floor, carefully glancing at each doorway to note the name of the resident who lived there. Each door had a gold nameplate and all nameplates had a name—unless of course no resident lived there. However, that happened seldom because when a resident moved away or died (the last option being the more common), the suites were quickly filled by new residents. Happy Haven was a popular assisted living facility and many older people wanted to live there.

As she rounded the corner at the end of the hallway, she found what she was looking for—Bob Weiderley's apartment, immediately on her left. Unfortunately, on his door was also a massive metal lock—the kind the police place on doors at crime scenes.   She realized that they had probably placed this external lock on Bob's door so that no one (and "no one" meant aides, cleaning people, or residents) could get into his apartment while he was in the hospital.  She remembered that she had seen a similar lock on her neighbor Charlene's door when Charlene was in rehab for several weeks after breaking her leg.  It took a special key to open the external lock and she had no idea where to find it.  She rolled her walker around and sat on its built-in seat.  Then she bent down to examine the structure of the lock, with the idea that possibly she could use a knife or a bobby pin to pry it open.  A shadow appeared.

"What are you doing?"    Essie popped upright, startled. Standing in front of her, hands on hips, was Violet Hendrickson, Director of Happy Haven.

"Violet!  Miss Hendrickson!" sputtered Essie.  "I . . . I . . . was just curious about these . . . locks.  I just saw it on this door and wondered how it worked.  You know, how it was attached and how it kept people from getting in."

"This isn't your room, Essie," said the tall woman, ignoring Essie's excuses.  She tapped her manicured fingertip on the sleeve of her beautiful purple designer suit coat.

"I know," replied Essie, blushing.  "I was just out for some exercise.  You know, Miss Hendrickson.  You always tell us how important it is to get some daily exercise . . ."

"That doesn't explain why you're trying to remove the lock from Mr. Weiderley's door," continued the Director, with no sign of warmth or understanding on her severe but carefully made up face.

"Oh, no, Miss Hendrickson!" said Essie.  "I'm certainly not trying to remove it!  I know how important it is to keep poachers out.  I was just looking to see how it works.  You know, how one could devise some sort of lock to place over a doorknob that would secure a door from outside.  Really quite inventive!"

"That's why we use them," responded Violet Hendrickson. "They're quite strong—and fool-proof.  You can't remove one without the key."

"That's wonderful!" noted Essie, stuttering. "Really, wonderful! I'd hate to see anyone break into Mr. Weiderley's apartment while the poor man is stuck in the hospital. He's such a nice gentleman. All of the ladies at my table admire him so much, we all . . ."

"That's fine, Essie," interrupted Violet, with a deep intake of air, "but that's enough curiosity for now, I believe. Why don't you get going and finish your walk."

"Oh, yes, ma'am. I'll do that!" Essie grabbed the handles of her walker, and guided it around and back down the main residential hallway of the second floor. When she reached the elevator, she risked a glance backwards. Violet Hendrickson was still standing there, staring at her.

## Chapter Eight

*"To be happy, we must be true to nature and carry our age along with us."*
—William Hazlitt

Back on the main floor, Essie exited the elevator to find Marjorie seated in the family room in front of the television with several other residents. She caught her friend's eye and gestured for her to follow her. Essie rolled her walker to a table near the back of the family room and parked. Marjorie soon arrived and docked her vehicle nearby as the two women pulled out chairs with their backs facing the rest of the residents on the other side of the family room.

"I didn't find Bob's room," reported Marjorie.

"I did," countered Essie, "and that's not all! Violet found me!"

"She was in Bob's room?" asked her pert, red-headed friend.

"No!" said Essie, shushing Marjorie. "She caught me trying to break into Bob's apartment."

"What?"

"And I would have gotten in too—and Violet would have been none the wiser, but they put one of those security locks on his doorknob!"

"Oh my!" gasped Marjorie. "And you were trying to pick the lock?"

"I didn't have a chance!" added Essie. "Old eagle-eye Hendrickson must have been lurking around just waiting for someone to break into Bob's place."

"Oh, Essie," scoffed Marjorie, "I think that's unlikely. She was just probably passing by. You know she tends to make a lot of unscheduled visits. I think she's checking up on the aides and the workers."

"Yeah, probably wants to make sure she squeezes every penny of work out of them," added Essie. "That woman scares me. The way she stares at you down her long, skinny nose. And those eyes. It's like they're little radar machines following you and your thoughts. I feel creepy when she looks at me, like she's looking right inside my head."

"What did you say when she caught you?"

"I think I mumbled and bumbled well enough. At least, she let me go with a warning. But I'll have to be really careful that I stay clear of her the next time. If she catches me anywhere near Bob's apartment again, I'll be in really big trouble."

"I know what you mean," Marjorie said. "Once I threw a candy wrapper in the trash bin outside the dining hall and I missed and it fell on the ground. It felt like someone was staring at me and when I looked around, there was Violet standing in the door of her office glaring at me and the wrapper on the ground. So I quickly bent over—well, as quickly as I can bend over—and picked it up and put it in the waste bin. She gave me this anemic little grin and then went back into her office. She scares me too."

" Good gravy train, Marjorie! Just listen to us! We sound like a couple of school kids who've been caught jumping in mud puddles. Why should we be scared of Violet? We're both adults. We have nothing to be scared of."

"Actually, you do, Essie," noted Marjorie. "I didn't do anything wrong. If I'd found Bob's apartment door with a padlock on it, I surely wouldn't have tried to break in."

"You're such a goody three shoes."

"Two shoes."

"I don't care how many shoes you wear, Marjorie!" sputtered Essie, trying to keep her voice low. She turned back to see if any of the other residents in the family room were paying any attention to their conversation. "The point is, we have to get inside Bob's room."

"How? We can't break open a padlock!"

"Not if we can get the key," suggested Essie, her eyes twinkling.

"Essie!" exclaimed Marjorie. "Just where do you think you're going to get the key to that lock?"

"I don't know," replied the feisty woman. "Obviously there has to be a key. One of the workers has to have it and probably more than one must know where it is."

"What about the worker who cleans Bob's apartment? Would that person have the key? Or know where it is?"

"Probably," answered Essie.

"Then we need to ask Opal. She probably knows the second floor workers better than we do."

"You're right. I'm not going to bother her now, but we'll ask her at supper."

"But, Essie. I just don't think it's wise to do this. They put that security lock on Bob's apartment for a reason. To keep people out—and that means you."

"Marjorie, I'm trying to help Bob. They have that lock there to prevent theft. I'm not going to steal any of Bob's prized possessions. I just want to look for something that might have upset him yesterday—upset him so much that he collapsed. You don't really think that Violet or any of the aides or workers at Happy Haven would actually go to that extent to help Bob, do you?"

"No," replied Marjorie, chewing on her small lower lip.

"Good," Essie said, standing. "Now, I have to get to my room asap if I don't want a major bladder event to happen right here in the family room. Need I say more?"

"No, actually, I'm in the same boat, Essie. I'll see you at supper." With that, the two women and their wheeled chargers maneuvered expertly out of the family room and back towards their own hallways and their own rooms. Essie arrived at her doorway and scooted into her bathroom just in time. *Blessed relief,* she thought. *Hmmph! Field trip to the botanical gardens, forget it! It's all I can do to get from the lobby to my own bathroom. What would I do if I had to find a toilet on the outdoor grounds of Reardon's botanical gardens? It would be horrible— embarrassing and uncomfortable.*

Sitting there in bliss, she looked up behind her at the shelving above her toilet. She couldn't help but notice several boxes of products designed for such delicate situations. Her daughter Prudence kept bringing different brands of pads over for her to try. That's why she had such a collection stacked up. There were thick ones and thin ones, short ones and long ones, scented ones and plain ones. There were pads that tucked and ones that didn't. But it all boiled down to one thing. They were all diapers and she was not going to be caught dead wearing a diaper. *Hell's cowbells*! she thought. The people who invented those things obviously didn't use them. Who wanted to walk around all day with wet pants? Well, she wasn't a baby and she didn't plan on spending one single minute wearing a diaper. No, she'd get to her bathroom (or some bathroom) when nature called and that was all there was to it.

Luckily, now that she had her little wheeled walker, she could move like the wind. She remembered when she'd had a wheel-less walker years ago. It was much slower going. She loved her new, sleek, little red wheeled number. It was surely the Ferrari of walkers. She could go really fast in it—and at times—like now—she needed to do just that.

Finished with her task, Essie pulled up her comfy pants and trousers. After washing her hands, she headed out into her apartment with her trusty wheeled steed. She plopped herself down into her favorite armchair and—taking a cue from Fay—promptly fell asleep.

## Chapter Nine

*"Experience is simply the name we give our mistakes."*
—Oscar Wilde

"Residents!" sang out the intercom, prying Essie from her slumber. "Residents, don't forget that after dinner tonight, our favorite ventriloquist Geoffrey George will be here with his pals Ducky and Doozy to perform for you in the lobby. You won't want to miss the fun! Seven sharp. Also, don't forget to sign up for the field trip to the botanical gardens at the front desk. Only three slots left. You won't want to miss the beautiful roses in bloom. Also, anyone who might have seen Agnes Woolwhistle's gold-handled cane, please report to the front desk."

"Heavens to hollyhocks!" declared Essie, rousing from her nap. "Agnes Woolwhistle is always losing her cane. Someone ought to tie it around her neck." Then, glancing at her wristwatch, she rubbed her eyes and pushed herself up from her chair. "Where did the afternoon go? I thought I just closed my eyes for a second."

Essie knew that the evening announcements signaled the start of the supper hour. She stood and straightened out her trousers and pulled up her socks which had rolled around her ankles like little donuts. "I guess that's enough primping," she said to herself, and, grabbing onto her walker, she headed out her front door and down the hallway towards the dining hall. As she got closer, she could see that Fay, Marjorie, and Opal were already in line. She pushed her machine faster and joined them at the back of the line.

"I understand you had quite a little adventure today," said Opal with a grimace. "Marjorie tells me you're on Violet's blacklist now."

"Hoot galoot, Marjorie! Can't you keep your mouth shut?" said Essie to her shorter friend as they waited for the line to move into the dining room. The residents dined in shifts and the four friends had the first shifts for all three meals. It was now five o'clock. As the waiter at the door opened the entrance, the line of residents piled through on their canes, walkers, and wheelchairs. Essie led the other three women across the dining hall to their regular table where they each took their regular seats. This consistency made the wait staff's job much easier.

"I managed to divert Violet's suspicions," Essie explained to Opal when they were all seated. "I was appropriately obsequious."

"I assume that means you apologized for trying to break into Bob's apartment!" said Opal, who apparently had been holding in her annoyance.

"Actually, Opal," said Essie, "I couldn't break in, even if Violet hadn't caught me, because they'd put one of those security locks on his front door."

"They always do that when a resident is gone from the building for a day or more," said Opal.

"I remember once I saw one of those strange locks on someone's door in my hallway," offered Marjorie, excited, "and I had no idea what it was for."

"Now you know!" said Essie, annoyed. She returned her attention to Opal. "All we had intended to do this afternoon, Opal, was to find out where Bob's apartment was—and we did that. He's on the second floor on the hallway to the left as you exit the elevator. You go all the way to the end and then turn left again. Bob's room is the first door on the left."

"I don't know why you're telling me this, Essie," huffed Opal. "They've locked his door, so I'm certainly not going to join you in trying to break into Bob Weiderley's room."

"No one is going to break into his place," said Essie with a shrug.

"Good," said Opal. "I'm glad to hear you've given up on this ridiculous plan."

"Oh, I haven't given up!" declared Essie. "I'm just using a different method."

"What method?" asked Marjorie, obviously still excited from the afternoon's adventure.

"Now that we know where Bob's room is and now that we know there is a security lock on his door," she detailed her idea to the women, "we need to find the key to the lock."

A waiter—not Santos—but a new (to them) older man arrived at their table and took their orders with little fanfare. The women spent little time deciding their choices from the menus as the offerings remained similar from one day to another. When he had gone, the discussion again returned to the situation with the security lock on Bob's apartment door.

"What I need to find out is where they keep the keys to this lock," announced Essie.

"Wouldn't the cleaning people have them?" Marjorie asked.

"If there's only one key for each lock," explained Essie, "then the cleaning people couldn't keep it all the time. I mean, what if it's on someone's door and one of their relatives needs to get inside the apartment?"

"But Bob doesn't have any relatives," argued Marjorie.

"I'm speaking hypothetically," retorted Essie.

"I know that when Herman Anspach was hospitalized several months ago, they had one of those things on his door. Once I saw his daughter taking it off of his door when she dropped by to pick up some of his clothes," said Opal, warming to the subject matter. "Surely, there must be a key for each security lock and they must keep them somewhere centrally located so that when family members come and need to get into a resident's place, someone can let the family member in—or give them a key so they can let themselves in."

"Yes, exactly!" said Essie, pointing her finger at Opal with glee. "I knew you'd know how all this must work. Now the question is where do they keep the keys to these security locks?"

The older waiter returned with their salads, beverages, and a basket of rolls.

"Roll!" yelled Fay, and Essie chose a particularly crispy looking one from the basket and handed it to her.

The other three women nibbled at their salads and sipped their drinks.

"I don't know," said Opal, continuing to chew the carrots in her salad.

"I wonder how many of these locks they have all together?" asked Marjorie.

"Good question," noted Essie, as she swallowed her tea. "They'd need enough to cover however many residents might be out for any particular number of days."

"And how many do you think that would be?" asked Opal.

"How many do you think? You're the one with the math background." Essie directed this to Opal who had spent her career as an administrative assistant doing balance sheets and inventories.

"That's not a math question. Even so, I'm guessing with the number of residents at Happy Haven—around 300—and the number of them who might feasibly be away at any one time, I'm guessing they'd have at least five, but probably no more than ten."

"That sounds about right to me," agreed Essie.

"Me too," said Marjorie.

"Me too," said Fay, her mouth full of roll. The other three women chuckled, wondering if Fay had any idea what she was "me-tooing."

"So what does that prove?" asked Opal.

"This is what I'm thinking," said Essie in a whisper. "Once they put these locks on a resident's door, they would have to have the key available in a convenient spot in case a family member showed up suddenly and needed to get into the apartment. That's why I'm guessing they must keep them—the locks and the keys— at the front desk. You know Phyllis has all sorts of stuff on that desk of hers behind the counter. There's the back room too. Here's what I'm thinking. They probably keep the unused locks and their keys in the back room, but they probably keep the keys for the locks that are in use on Phyllis's desk."

"Makes sense," agreed Marjorie.

"She has little boxes with paper clips and erasers in them. I think she has a little basket on her desk and I think I've seen small keys in there," said Opal.

"What I wouldn't give to be tall like you, Opal," said Essie. "I can never see over that counter for love or lipstick."

"How many keys have you seen in it?" asked Marjorie.

"I can't remember," said Opal. "It's not like I had any interest in the doodads on her desk. Just a lot of junk, if you ask me."

"Think, Opal," urged Essie. "I mean, were there dozens? Hundreds? What?"

"No, no!" replied the tall, stern woman. "Just a few. I think each one had a little brightly colored tag on the end—I think—with a number."

"It's probably how they keep the locks and the keys matched together. Yes! That must be it!" said Essie.

"So what?" asked Opal. "What good does it do us to know that they keep these keys at the front desk?"

"We can't just have you grab all of them," mused Essie.

"Me!" screeched Opal. "Why me?"

"Because you're the only one tall enough to reach over the counter!" said Marjorie. "Keep up, Opal!"

"Quiet!" said Essie calmly.

The old waiter arrived with their main courses and they curtailed their discussion until he left.

"What?" whispered Opal. "What wild caper do you have planned now, Essie? Something to jeopardize my residence here at Happy Haven?"

"No," said Essie, "you can't just go up to the front desk and grab all the security lock keys."

"Thank God!" said Opal, taking a deep breath. "For a minute I thought you were going to appoint me your hit man."

"I think you mean front man," suggested Marjorie.

"Oh, you will be the most important part of this plot, Opal," said Essie, "but not quite yet. First, I need to do some reconnaissance."

"What?" replied both Opal and Marjorie.

"You said the keys are color coded? Right?" Essie asked Opal.

"Yes, if I remember correctly," said Opal.

"Then, what I need to do is sneak back up to Bob's apartment and check to see what the matching color is on the security lock. Surely if the keys are color coded to the locks, the locks must have the matching color marked on them somewhere. Once we know the appropriate color of Bob's lock, then Opal, you can go grab the correct colored key from Phyllis's desk."

"Essie, are you crazy?" said Opal. "She'll see me!"

"Not if Marjorie and I are right there to distract her," said Essie. She smiled with her hands stretched out palms up, and a look on her face that said it was obvious.

"How about dessert?" asked the old waiter as he stumbled around their table picking up their plates. Where was Santos? Essie wondered.

"None for me," said Essie, "but I would like some more coffee. I need to be wide awake tonight."

"Oh, yes," said the old man, smiling. "The ventriloquist! Ducky and Doozy! Everyone says he's quite marvelous."

"Yes," agreed Essie with a small smirk. "Ducky and Doozy."

"Ducky and Doozy," said Marjorie and Opal, both nodding knowingly at each other.

"Coffee all around!" Essie said.

"Yes, ma'am," said the waiter as all four women nodded in his direction.

"Ducky and Doozy!" shouted Fay several beats after the coffee had been poured.

The old waiter gave a skeptical shrug and carted the four dinner plates back to the kitchen.

## Chapter Ten

*"I'm not interested in age. People who tell me their age are silly. You're as old as you feel."*
—Elizabeth Arden

They were now all hanging around the lobby. Opal had seen to it that Fay had made it back to her room and then she returned. Then Essie made Marjorie and Opal wait while she went somewhere.

"Now, where did she go?" asked Opal.

"To check on the you-know-what of the you-know-what," responded Marjorie.

"Oh, of course," replied Opal, looking confused.

Within ten minutes, Essie had returned. She plopped herself back down between the women and whispered one word: "yellow."

Then the three women rolled their walkers to the front desk. Phyllis, the front desk clerk, was speaking with an elderly gentleman. He was asking about an upcoming trip—not the infamous botanical gardens one; it sounded like he was discussing a shopping trip. Happy Haven frequently took residents out for shopping at outlet malls or grocery stores. Some residents liked to keep some of their favorite foods in their small refrigerators in their apartments. Of course, none of them needed to buy food because anything they might want was supplied to them in the dining hall.

"Yes, sir," said Phyllis, a soft-spoken, gentle lady, to the man, "the outlet mall trip is Saturday. The grocery store trip is Wednesday. That's the way it is every week."

"I need to get some milk," he demanded in a high-pitched, squeaky voice.

"I'm sure they'll give you whatever milk you need in the dining hall," she said, consoling.

"I need a container of milk," he insisted. "I need it for early in the morning, before the dining hall opens."

"I understand, sir," repeated Phyllis. "I'm sure the dining hall staff will be happy to give you a container of milk. Just go back into the kitchen and ask them."

"Oh, all right," he snapped at her finally as if he'd been asked to climb Everest. He shuffled off towards the dining hall.

"Now, ladies," said Phyllis, turning toward Essie and smiling at the women, "what can I do for you?" Essie and Marjorie moved to the far right end of the counter as the women had discussed they would do, and Opal moved discreetly towards the far left end. As Essie and Marjorie engaged Phyllis in discussion, Opal leaned over the top of the counter and scanned Phyllis's desk for the basket of keys that she had vaguely remembered seeing.

"I was wondering if you could tell us about the field trip to the botanical gardens," said Essie. Marjorie nodded behind her.

"Oh, yes!" said Phyllis. "It's a very popular trip! We've only got three slots left."

"How long does it take?" asked Marjorie.

"I believe the group is usually gone around three hours from the time they leave until the time they return," said Phyllis.

Opal was leaning over the counter, her left arm dangling— supposedly inconspicuously—onto Phyllis's desk.

"What about bathroom breaks?" asked Essie, which was the primary question as far as she was concerned.

"Oh, dear," laughed Phyllis, "I'm sure there are plenty of restrooms at the gardens. We've had our residents visiting there for years and I know they always find the restrooms."

"How would you know?" asked Essie. Opal's arm moved around and Essie could hear a slight jingly noise coming from the other end of the counter.

"Me?" said Phyllis. "Well, I don't know for sure. I've never been there myself, but I'm sure . . ."

"So you've never actually seen any bathrooms at this botanical gardens place," accused Essie, her nose aiming at Phyllis's face like an arrow.

There was more jostling of desk items from Opal. Marjorie cringed. Essie spoke up even louder.

"What if I have to use the toilet while I'm still on the bus?" demanded Essie.

"Oh, you won't be on the bus but maybe fifteen minutes or so, Essie. The gardens are fairly close."

"When I have to go, my bladder won't hold for fifteen minutes!" pronounced Essie. Phyllis looked at the two women with a combination of dread and humor.

Opal surreptitiously held up a small gold key in front of her face so that Essie and Marjorie could see it, then quickly palmed it and moved closer to the women.

"I'm sure you'd be just fine!" insisted Phyllis. At that point, Sue Barber, the Social Director who had participated in Bob Weiderley's care during his Bingo collapse, approached the group from the office wing.

"Ladies," she said warmly, "I couldn't help but overhear your discussion."

"Miss Barber," said Phyllis with some relief, "these ladies are interested in the botanical gardens field trip."

"Wonderful!" cried Sue Barber. "Three of you! And just three spots left! Here!" She grabbed the sign-up sheet and held out a pen towards Essie. "Essie, I know you want to go, our flower and plant expert!" She pushed the pen into Essie's hand and pointed to the empty line on the sheet. Essie gulped and looked from Marjorie to Opal, receiving absolutely no support. With a grimace, she signed her name.

"Wonderful!" sung Sue. "I know you'll have a wonderful time! Now, your turn, Marjorie. Surely you will want to join your friend." Marjorie quickly grabbed the pen and added her signature below Essie's. After that, Opal (with the gold key in her left hand) signed below Marjorie with her right hand.

"This is absolutely wonderful!" announced Sue. "We now have a busload for the field trip. I'm just delighted!"

"I'll probably have to pee as soon as I get on the bus," whined Essie.

"Oh, you can hold it, Essie," said Sue. "If anyone can, you can!" She gave each of the three women a quick, imperceptible hug and then practically skipped off towards her office which was next door to Violet's.

As soon as Sue Barber had disappeared from view, the three ladies waved goodbye to Phyllis and pushed their walkers towards the fireplace where they seated themselves in a group.

"Did you get it?" asked Essie.

"Right here," said Opal, holding her hand low and out to Essie, then carefully pulling her fingers back so that Essie and Marjorie could see the small, yellow-marked key.

"Now what?" asked Marjorie.

"Now we break into Bob's apartment," said Essie with determination. She started to rise.

"Wait a minute, Essie," said Opal, stopping her by her sleeve. "Don't you think we should plan this through before we go off half-cocked?"

"What's to plan? We take the lock off his door, go inside, and search around to see if there's anything there that might explain why he was so upset last night," said Essie.

Several residents sat down across from them and the women lowered their voices. More residents entered the lobby and placed themselves in chairs around the periphery. Some even sat on the edge of the fireplace.

"First of all," Opal said quietly, "are all three of us going to do this?"

"Why not?" shrugged Essie. "One of us can stand watch at the door and the other two can search."

"That sounds like a good idea," agreed Marjorie.

Sue Barber walked by Essie's chair, making her cringe. She'd have to get out of that field trip, she mused. Then immediately, she returned to considering the break-in at Bob's apartment.

"What kinds of things are we looking for?" asked Opal.

"I don't know," said Essie, "but since whatever it was that caused Bob to be so upset happened right recently, it's probably something that we'll find out in plain sight. I mean, if it's tucked away at the bottom of a closet, it probably isn't something that just came to Bob's attention. . ."

"Attention!" called Sue Barber.

*Now what*? thought Essie. They were trying to work out the particulars of this plan and here Sue Barber was again sticking her nose into the middle of things.

"Attention, residents!" called Sue. "I'm delighted to introduce to you tonight's special guest. The world renowned ventriloquist, Geoffrey George, with his friends Ducky and Doozy!"

Applause filled the lobby as a tall, gangly clown with loud striped pants and floppy shoes entered from the office wing holding two large, weird dummies—Ducky and Doozy, obviously. Geoffrey George walked in front of the fireplace—and immediately before Essie, Marjorie, and Opal—making their exit virtually impossible. He held up the dummies. Ducky—or possibly Doozy—had the first comment.

"Welcome, boys and girls!"

The room erupted with laughter. Doozy—or possibly Ducky—interrupted his pal.

"They're not boys and girls! They're ladies and gentlemen!"

"I like the lady with the red hair!" noted one of the D's and gave an audible sigh as he leaned (or rather Geoffrey George held him) towards Marjorie. Marjorie smiled sweetly at the creature and then quickly rose from her seat and planted a big kiss on its nose. The puppet flipped over and landed upside down on his back, all the while clutching his heart which was supposedly beating so hard he had to hold it inside his chest.

The crowd went wild. *Great*, thought Essie, *now we'll never get out of here*. And she was right. A good hour later, the great Geoffrey George and Ducky and Doozy had completed their act and had thoroughly enchanted each and every resident of Happy Haven—every resident that is, except Essie Cobb. The puppets and their master were now holding court in the dining hall, having strawberry shortcake (those ultra-large berries promised in the morning by Santos) and surrounded by a bevy of delighted ladies and a few men.

Essie kept her group—Marjorie and Opal—in the lobby. It was a lot later than she had intended to get started. But the sooner they got into Bob's apartment, Essie reasoned. the sooner they'd know what was going on.

"Actually," said Essie to her two friends, "this ventriloquist might work to our advantage. It looks like most of the residents are in the dining hall talking to him. Hopefully, that means they won't be roaming the halls on the second floor."

"Are we really going through with this, Essie?" asked Marjorie.

"Why not?" replied Essie.

"Did we ever decide exactly how we're going about this?" asked Opal. "Personally, I'd rather be the look-out. I just don't feel right snooping in somebody's personal effects."

"I don't mind looking around," said Marjorie, "but I don't want to go through his underwear drawer or his personal man-type items in his bathroom."

"Like what?" queried Essie.

"You know, Essie. Things that men have that are embarrassing," she said.

"Like razors and shaving cream?" asked Essie.

"No, you know, things he might have in a drawer for—you know—sex," whispered Marjorie with a squeamish look on her face.

"Oh, Joan's bones!" exclaimed Essie, "you had a husband, Marjorie. It's not like you never saw . . ."

"Enough!" said Opal, "Marjorie, if you run across something distasteful just call Essie! Nothing bothers her!"

"That's fine. Do that," agreed Essie, "but I hardly think that Bob collapsed at Bingo and is now lying in the hospital in a coma because someone found his condoms! Let's be sensible. This is serious and we need to conduct a serious search."

"All right," said Marjorie. "I'm ready."

"I'm ready too," said Opal.

"Then let's get going before it's past our bedtimes," said Essie, with a look of grim determination on her tanned, wrinkled and very determined face.

## Chapter Eleven

*"I refuse to admit I'm more than fifty-two, even if that does make my sons illegitimate."*
—Lady Nancy Astor

The far end of the left second floor hallway was quiet, really quiet for eight o'clock on a week night. It was as if all the residents were downstairs in the dining hall talking to a ventriloquist and his dummies. Three heads peeked around the corner. Nothing stirred in the far end of the back hallway.

"Give me the key, Opal," said Essie. Opal reached out her left hand and dropped the tiny gold key into Essie's palm.

Essie moved cautiously towards Bob's apartment door. Marjorie followed. Opal remained at the corner, continuing to keep watch down the main hallway in case anyone should arrive by the elevator at the other end and begin the long trek down the corridor and the back hallway that ran perpendicular to the main one. Essie and Marjorie moved towards Bob's door. The large security lock remained attached to the doorknob. Essie took the key and moved the security lock around until she found the keyhole. Then she inserted the key and twisted until the lock popped audibly, causing the device to separate into two parts in her hands. Essie handed the separated security lock parts to Marjorie while she turned the door handle.

The door to Bob Weiderley's apartment opened easily but with some noise. Essie entered cautiously into the darkened room that had a floor plan much like her own. Marjorie followed behind, giving Opal a nod just before she closed the door behind herself.

Inside, Essie ran her hand over the right hand wall until she found the light switch. She hit one of the buttons and immediately there was light from several lamps in the small living room. Bob had laid out his living room much like Essie's except he had a much larger desk directly across from the door underneath his living room window. His bedroom and bathroom were off to the right as they were in Essie's (and probably Marjorie's apartment) too.

"Marjorie," said Essie, "I'm going to go through his kitchen and living room. You work on the bedroom and bathroom."

"Okay, Essie," agreed Marjorie, "but if I find anything disgusting, I'm coming out here to get you."

"Fine!"

Marjorie deposited the security lock and key on the sink and then headed off to the right and Essie went immediately to work on the small kitchen or nook. She opened the cabinet doors and all the drawers. Inside, all she found were garbage bags, dishwashing detergent, a few plates, cups, and some silverware. Inside of Bob's small refrigerator were some staples, but nothing unusual.

She then moved into the living room. She checked underneath the cushions of the chairs and the long sofa. There was a *TV Guide* on the sofa but that was all. There was no telephone in the living room. Bob must be one of those individuals who had one of those cell phones, she thought. Maybe Marjorie would find a telephone in the bedroom. There was a magazine rack beside the sofa. In it were some sporting magazines and a few political magazines, but nothing of a personal nature.

She continued across the room to what appeared to be the center of attention—a large desk. This was more a businessman's desk than a home desk. On the top was a blotter, a small calendar, several in- and out-files, and boxes full of papers. The long drawer in the front of the desk held paraphernalia such as erasers, glue, scotch tape, paper clips, etc. The side desk drawers held hanging files all neatly labeled and alphabetized. Everything on the desk was neat and everything appeared to be put away. This was certainly Bob's desk because it was as neat and organized as he was—at least it seemed that way to Essie.

On the desk blotter laid an envelope addressed to Bob. It was postmarked yesterday. The return address was from a Ben Jericho at 1224 Waterford Way in a small town not at all close to Reardon. There was a letter inside. The envelope had been opened. Essie guessed that the letter inside had probably been read and then returned to the envelope by Bob. Essie wondered about the meaning of that.

As she removed the letter, Marjorie came back into the living room, her walker scraping against the carpet.

"Essie, there just isn't anything anywhere," she claimed. "I looked through his bath items—nothing there. Not very much in his medicine cabinet above the sink either—just some vitamins and some bottles of herbal supplements. A few bottles of prescription drugs, but I don't know what they're for. There's nothing in his bed stand—not even anything sex-related. I even looked under the bed—and the mattress! Bob just isn't very interesting." She stood in the middle of the living room, tapping her fingers on the handles of her walker.

"Hang on, Marjorie," said Essie. "There's a letter here I want to read."

"Is it important?" asked Marjorie, inching closer to the desk.

"I don't know," said Essie. "I just found it lying here on the desk. It appears he just got it yesterday."

"Oh, that sounds weird," said Marjorie.

"Maybe yes, maybe no," agreed Essie. "It might just be a coincidence. I need to read it first."

At that moment, the front door opened and Opal rolled quickly inside and just as quickly turned and shut the door behind her.

"There's a woman I don't know coming down the main hallway," she announced.

"Where's the lock?" asked Essie.

"Here," said Marjorie rolling back and grabbing the item from the sink.

"Let's all go into the bedroom, just in case," she whispered.

They all rolled their walkers, twisting their vehicles expertly around the bedroom doorframe (something they had learned to do in their own apartments which were identical to this one) until they were all in Bob's bedroom. Essie shut the bedroom door.

Almost immediately there was a knock on Bob's main door.

"Bob?" called out a female voice from the hallway. "Bob, are you back? Are you back from the hospital?"

The women remained frozen as the unknown woman continued knocking and calling to Bob. After a few moments, they heard the front doorknob turn and the front door open.

Sounds of footsteps indicated that the woman, whoever she was, had moved slightly inside the door.

"Bob, are you home?" she called out. "Bob, did they release you from the hospital? I was just checking on you."

The unknown woman stood there a while and waited. The three women hiding in the bedroom were frozen in silence. Finally, the woman in the living room gave an audible sigh and turned and left, closing the front door behind her. After a few minutes, when they were fairly certain she was gone for good, the three friends returned to the living room from the bedroom.

"What was that?" asked Marjorie, hanging over her walker and panting.

"I'm guessing she was a friend of Bob's—maybe Hazel or Rose or Evelyn, one of his tablemates--who for some reason thought that he was home from the hospital," suggested Opal, as she nervously rolled her walker back and forth.

"She evidently didn't hear that he's in a COMA!" shrieked Essie in a whispered scream.

"I know," said Marjorie. "She must have seen that the lock wasn't on his door! She walks by this door all the time and had seen the lock here when she knew he'd been taken to the hospital. Then tonight, she walks by and there's no security lock! So, all of a sudden, she assumes that he's better and that he's returned home and back in his apartment."

"That's it!" agreed Essie. "What a close call! I don't know how we'd explain ourselves if she'd found us."

"Much more easily than we would explain ourselves if Violet found us!" noted Opal, shaking her head.

"You're right," said Marjorie, "Can we get out of here, Essie?"

"Yes, let's get going," agreed Essie. "I'll read this letter when I get back to my place."

Essie slipped the letter in the envelope under the seat of her walker which contained a nice compartment for carrying things. Then the threesome carefully checked outside the doorway before entering the hallway. Essie slipped the security lock back on Bob's front doorknob and, using the small gold key, locked it back in place. Opal then took the key and the three ladies rolled quietly to the corner of the main hallway. Carefully checking around the corner and seeing no one in sight, they turned onto the main second floor corridor and headed to the elevator. When they reached the elevator, the door was just opening. They passed several residents exiting who had obviously just returned from visiting with Geoffrey George because they were still talking about Ducky and Doozie. Essie and Marjorie and Opal entered the elevator. When they were alone inside the compartment, they all breathed a sigh of relief. On the main floor, Essie led her two friends to her apartment (after a quick stop at the front desk where Opal discreetly returned the gold key).

Inside Essie's apartment, the women sat in Essie's living room and Essie removed the envelope that she had taken from Bob Weiderley's desk from under her walker seat.

"It's from a Ben Jericho and it was postmarked yesterday" explained Essie.

"And the postman delivers the mail in the afternoon," said Marjorie.

"Yes, mail is usually put in our boxes mid-afternoon," said Essie. Then, she slapped her forehead with her hand.

"What?" asked Opal.

"When I asked Fay what she thought Bob was upset about. . ."

"You asked Fay, Essie?" queried Marjorie.

"She probably doesn't even know Bob is in the hospital," added Opal.

"Yes," continued Essie, "but when I asked her, she said 'box' and she said it twice. Don't you find that strange? Maybe she does know something.  Maybe she knows he got a letter in his mail box that upset him."

"I doubt it," argued Marjorie.  "What could she know?  She sleeps through the day."

"But she did beat us at Canasta this morning!" noted Essie.

"That was a fluke!" said Opal.

"Never mind," said Essie, "let's just figure out what to do about this letter."

"If Bob read this letter yesterday afternoon," suggested Opal, "then it's quite likely the reason he was so upset at supper."

"Yes!" said Marjorie, "it must be the reason!"

"Let's find out, shall we?" said Essie.  She opened the letter. Inside were two pages of handwritten prose and a photograph of a man.  There was nothing on the back of the picture.

"Read it!" ordered Marjorie.

"Okay," said Essie.  "It's addressed 'Dear Mr. Weiderley.'" Essie began to read.  "This letter may come as a shock to you. . ."

"Oh, no!" said Marjorie.  "A shock!"

"This letter may come as a shock to you, or it may not.  You may not even believe it, but I assure you everything I tell you is true."

"No wonder poor Bob was so upset at supper.  Just the opening petrifies me," said Opal.

"My name is Ben Jericho.  I have a good life—a wife and three wonderful children.  My father died over ten years ago.  He was a wonderful man and I miss him terribly.  I was lucky that my mother was in good health until just recently.  Last year, my mother became quite ill.  She realized that she didn't have much time left.  Several weeks before she died, she called me to her home to discuss something with me.  I thought it would be about burial arrangements or something she wanted done at her funeral. I was totally surprised when she told me that she'd been keeping a secret from me my entire life.  She realized that now that she was about to die, she owed it to me to tell me the truth.  I had absolutely no idea what she meant.  My mother then told me that the man I had considered to be my father all these years was actually not my father.

"She told me that when she was very young, right before World War II, she met a young soldier who was about to be shipped off. She felt sorry for him and was concerned about him and she decided to spend his last few days of freedom with him, trying to provide him with something to remember. She never intended for their time together to become intimate—but it did. And by the end of their three days together, she told me she had fallen deeply in love with this man—and, she believed, he with her. But, it didn't matter. He was shipped off to war—and she never heard from him again.

"A few months later, she met my father and they started dating. They became serious and when my mother realized that she was pregnant, she told my father what had happened with the soldier several months previous. Being the wonderful, gracious gentleman that he was, it didn't matter to my father. They were married and he raised me as his own son—which I was for all intents and purposes. They had a wonderful marriage. There was not only me, but eventually they had children of their own—my sister, and two other brothers.

"I miss my father and mother terribly. I was quite happy to let matters stand where they were. Unfortunately, my mother was not content to do that. When she realized that she was dying, she insisted that I try to find my biological father—the soldier she had fallen in love with before he left for war. She asked me to find him FOR her. She knew she would never live to see him. She didn't want to cause him any distress and she certainly didn't want me to cause him any distress, but she truly believed that I should know my real father.

"She told me his name. She said he would remember her. She said to tell him that she was the girl with the smiling eyes. Her maiden name was Julia Warren and she married Andrew Jericho. She said my real father's name was Bob Weiderley. "

"Oh my God!" cried Marjorie.

Essie continued reading.

"I have been looking for Bob Weiderley—my biological father. There are a few men named Bob Weiderley in the country, but not any that have all the criteria that my mother described. I believe I have found the correct Bob Weiderley—the Bob Weiderley that once upon a time loved my mother, Julia Warren. I believe that Bob Weiderley is you, sir. Mr. Weiderley, I believe I am your son—yours and Julia's.

I don't know your situation, Mr. Weiderley. I don't wish to disrupt your family or cause you any anguish. If you wish to communicate with me, we can do so without ever mentioning our situation to anyone else. I've enclosed a recent photograph of me. I hope you see yourself and my mother in my features. People have always said I look like my mother.

Sincerely,

Ben Jericho"

"Oh, my God!" exclaimed Marjorie. "No wonder Bob collapsed! Let me see his photo." Essie passed the small picture to her two friends.

"Do you think he looks like Bob?" asked Opal.

"I can't tell," responded Marjorie.

"The poor man!" added Opal.

"Poor man is right!" said Essie. "I say, this is all a crock of doo doo!"

"What?" screeched Marjorie, "this is the most romantic thing I've ever heard."

"Romantic," sneered Essie, "this man—this Ben Jericho—is after Bob's five million dollars!"

"Oh," said Marjorie, deflated. "I hadn't thought of that. Do you really think he'd do that? I mean, we didn't know that Bob was rich. How could this Jericho fellow find out about Bob's money?"

"Essie," added Opal, "you really believe that this man is playing some scam on Bob?"

"I'd bet money on it," said Essie, then added, "But I certainly wouldn't bet five million dollars!"

"Would Bob collapse just because he thought someone was trying to scam him?" asked Marjorie.

"But Essie, what this Jericho says in his letter just might be true," argued Opal.

"I doubt it.  Bob is a multi-millionaire and he's a lonely old man with no family.  He's the perfect target for such a scam," argued Essie.

"What are we going to do?" asked Marjorie.

"We're going to confront this Ben Jericho!" announced Essie. "But, first we're going to find out everything we can about him."

"How?" asked Opal.  "How can three old ladies track down some scam artist?"

"If he is a scam artist," said Marjorie.

"We can do what we do best," said Essie.  "Use our feminine wiles."

"What feminine wiles?" asked Opal.  "I'm not sure I ever had any and I'm quite sure I don't have any now."

"You sell yourself short, Opal," said Essie.  "It's just a matter of figuring out what we need to know and then finding it."

"Essie," said Marjorie, "it's after eight o'clock.  My aide will be by soon to give me my evening meds.  If I'm not in my room, she'll come looking for me."

"Me too," agreed Opal.  "It's hard to be a detective when you're so conspicuous."

"I know," agreed Essie.  "But, we can do it.  We just need to keep our eyes and ears open.  Let me think about this and we'll reconnoiter tomorrow."

"I assume that means something that doesn't involve a high speed chase," added Marjorie.

"If it does," said Essie with a wink, "just remember, we have the fastest speed walkers in the place!"

### Chapter Twelve

*"My idea of Hell is to be young again."*
—Marge Piercy

The next morning was cool but clear. Unfortunately, Essie's mind was not clear. She had tossed and turned all night long trying to figure out what—if anything—to do about the letter from the mysterious Ben Jericho that now resided on her nightstand like some ravenous, monster from the darkest reaches of Hell. As the sunlight poured into her living room, it illuminated the rectangle with its colorful stamp in the corner that she had placed on her end table next to her telephone. After DeeDee had helped her dress and given her her meds, she'd sat in her favorite chair and thought. *No crossword puzzle this morning for me*, she thought. As she had contemplated her options during her sleepless night, she had come to only a few conclusions. First, she had concluded that she was going to do something. That is, she wasn't going to just return the letter to Bob's room and pretend as if nothing had happened. She firmly believed that this letter was the event that had led to Bob's collapse and ultimately his coma. She knew she had to do something about it, but she didn't know exactly what.

What were her options? She could confess her theft and take the letter to Violet and let her deal with this Ben Jericho. No, that wouldn't work. Violet was strictly hands-off residents' private business. She would just chastise Essie for breaking into Bob's room, return the letter, and then do nothing about the scam artist Jericho. No, telling Violet or anyone else in authority was not an option. She—and Opal and Marjorie (and Fay)—would have to handle this themselves. But how?

As it was impossible to take the letter to Bob or discuss it with him (and she wasn't sure that she would do that even if Bob were not in a coma), it meant that she would have to find out if this Jericho's story of his birth as described in the letter was true. If it was true, well, then that would be Bob's concern if and when he recovered. If it was not true (which it probably wasn't), then maybe she could do something about it so that Bob would not have this one more thing to worry about when (if) he did come out of his coma.

*But how? How to track down Ben Jericho?* She knew his name, address, and town from the return address on the envelope. She had his photo. She had no phone number. Even if she could get his phone number from long distance information, she didn't believe she should confront him directly. That would give him an unnecessary advantage—to let him know that someone was on to him. She needed to find out what she could about him without him knowing what she was doing.

A small, niggling idea began to form in the back of her brain. *Hmmm.* She had to be careful and approach things carefully, she thought to herself. She would begin with a phone call. She reached for her appointment book and turned to the B's. Ned Brannigan was the name she was looking for, her grandson. Claudia's oldest son was some sort of computer wizard (so she was told) and now the CEO of his own computer firm. Claudia often gushed about his accomplishments whenever she visited Essie. A charming, outgoing young man, Ned had inherited Essie's vigor and cleverness, she thought, so she didn't feel as if asking for his assistance would be any imposition—even though it was 7:30 a.m.

"Hello, Ned," she spoke into her telephone receiver, probably a little louder than necessary. She always found it a bit hard to hear people on the other end. People tended to whisper when they spoke on the phone, she found. "Hello, Ned. This is your Grandma Essie."

"Grandma!" responded a cheerful voice. "Wow! It's early! I'm still in bed. Are you okay?"

"No, no!  I'm just fine," she laughed. "I'm calling you, Ned, because I need your help."

"Of course, Grandma," replied the young man. "What can I do? Something that Mom can't help you with?  Do you need me to move some furniture for you?"

"No," she said. "I need computer help!"

"Wow, Grandma!" chuckled Ned, "I sure wasn't expecting to hear you say that!  I thought you considered computers the Devil's instruments."

"No, no!" she said, "they're just way too fancy for me.  But, Ned, I have this friend, uh, friend here at Happy Haven who is having a problem.  I wonder if maybe you can advise me how to help this . . . friend with a computer question."

"I'll sure try, Grandma," responded Ned. "What's the problem?"

"I don't even know if it is a computer problem, but if it isn't, just tell me that too," she said.

"Okay," he laughed, "but almost anything can be a computer problem nowadays."

"Very well," she said. "My . . . friend is trying to find someone, someone who doesn't live here in town.  They want to find out information about this . . . uh, person, but they don't want to contact the person directly.  They have a name and address but no phone number.  Oh, and they have a photograph!  I don't know if that's important or not."

"It could be," suggested Ned. "And, Grandma, this is definitely a computer problem—one that probably has a fairly easy solution."

"Oh, good!" she responded with delight, thinking she had done the right thing by contacting her young grandson.

"I would simply tell your friend to Google this person," said Ned. "That should produce a search results page full of information—newspaper columns, online articles, and similar things about the person.  Some of those things may have photographs so your friend can verify the photo they have with the photos online."

"How do I tell my friend to do this Google thing?" she asked.

She could hear the gentle laughter over the phone line.

"If your friend is computer-literate . . ."

"I guess you mean if my friend uses a computer. He . . . I mean she doesn't."

"You know, Grandma," continued Ned, "I've been trying to get you to let me bring you a small laptop computer that you could use for photos and email and stuff . . ."

"Thank you, Ned, but I really don't need one of those things myself," she explained. "I just need to know what to tell my friend to do to find out about this person."

"Would you like me to come over there to Happy Haven and help your friend with an online search? I could come over later this afternoon."

"No, no!" she interjected. "My friend is . . . uh . . . sort of shy. Uh, she wouldn't like that. Let's just stick with this Google thing."

"You can have her do that on one of those two old clunkers they have in the family room at Happy Haven," he continued.

"I've never used those things, Ned," she said, cringing.

"I know, Grandma," he replied, and Essie could hear a little bit of a scolding coming on.

"Can you tell me what to do? So I can show my friend?"

"All right. Maybe you should write this down."

"No, no. I'll remember. Just tell me how to do the Google."

"Okay, first make sure the computer is turned on. Can you do that? Then, sign on to the Internet."

"How do I do that?"

"Grandma, you'd better let me come over and help you."

"I'll figure it out. Go on."

"Maybe someone there who actually uses the computers can help. Anyway, once you're on the Internet, you type in 'Google' which will take you to the Google home page. Here you will see a search box."

"A box," she replied. "I've got it."

"Just type in the person's name in the search box along with whatever other information you have like address and home town. Then hit 'enter' and you'll see a long list of items. If you click your mouse on each of these items, it will bring up pages about this person."

"These items are about the person?" she asked.

"Yes," he said, "some of the items may be newspaper articles about the person. They may be related to social or business aspects of the person's life."

"That's great! That's just what I . . . I mean, what my friend needs!"

"But, Grandma," cautioned Ned, "if you have any problems doing any of this, I would be more than happy to drop by your place and help you or set you up with your own unit."

"No thanks, Ned. I think I understand. Google, search box, click item with mouse. Thank you. Bye!"

"Uh, bye, Grandma."

Essie gently placed the receiver back in its cradle. Grabbing a pad of paper and a pencil, she quickly jotted down what she remembered of Ned's directions. She really didn't understand any of what he'd said but she hoped that when she and Marjorie and Opal sat down at one of the two computers in the family room, one of the three of them would be able to figure the directions out.

*Computers*, she thought. She had avoided the treacherous machines ever since they had appeared. Now it seemed she would have to make their acquaintance.

# Chapter Thirteen

*"Anyone who stops learning is old, whether at twenty or eighty."*
—Henry Ford

Several hours following breakfast, Essie and her three companions in detection were ensconced before one of the two large desktop computer consoles located along the back wall in the family room. Essie sat directly in front of the screen in her walker seat, having removed the rolling computer chair off to the side. Fay was to her right in her wheelchair, Opal was directly behind, and Marjorie sat on her left. All four women were bent close to the glowing computer screen, partially because they couldn't see it well and partially because they didn't want any passers-by to notice what they were doing.

"If anyone asks," said Essie, turning from one woman to another, "we're practicing our computer skills so we can learn to be emailers. I've heard that term and it seems like something we could all do."

"Email," they all agreed in a pact, including Fay.

"I hardly get any regular mail," noted Opal from behind Essie's chair, "so maybe getting some of this email is just what I need."

"We're not doing any email," explained Essie. "We're just using it as an excuse for all of us sitting here at this computer."

"Okay," said Marjorie, "let's get busy. What do we do first?"

Essie picked up her small notepad and ran her finger up to the first item on her list.

"First, we have to get on the Internet," she said.

"How do we do that?" asked Opal, bending over and peering intently at the colorful screen.

"Ned said something about a mouse," recalled Essie.

"I think that's the mouse," said Marjorie, pointing to the small round plastic device attached to a long cord next to the monitor. The mouse sat on a rubber pad that proclaimed "Happy Haven Assisted Living Facility."

"Oh," said Essie, touching the round plastic mouse cautiously. "Ooops!" As she touched it, the screen came to life and a white arrow appeared on the blue screen.

"Oh, my!" said Opal, applauding. "That was wonderful, Essie!" Essie quickly removed her hand from the device as if she'd been stung.

"No, Essie, don't let go!" directed Marjorie, "You have to hold on to it! Look, when you touched it, that little arrow popped up!"

"Do you think that arrow is pointing us to the Internet?" asked Essie.

As the three women argued about what to do next, Fay reached over from her wheelchair seat to the right of Essie and grabbed the mouse. Expertly using the mouse to slide the white arrow down a list of choices along the left-hand side of the screen, she stopped her hand movement at an entry that said "Internet."

"Look!" said Opal with a surprised cheer. "Fay's found the Internet!" And indeed, as soon as Fay clicked the link, the screen changed. Fay lifted her hand from the mouse and sat back in her seat smiling.

"How did you do that, Fay?" Essie asked the rosy-cheeked, smiling face to her right. Fay smiled even more broadly as the other three women were awed at her performance.

"It doesn't matter," said Marjorie, calling their attention back to the screen. "Look! It's the Google!"

And sure enough. On the screen, in large, primary colors, the words "Google" appeared at the top.

"Essie," said Opal, pointing at a rectangular-shaped box directly below the Google icon on the screen. "Look! It's a box!"

Essie glanced down at her notepad. Running her finger down the instructions that Ned had given her, she read, "type in name in search box."

"Hmm," she said to herself. "Do you think that's the search box? Ned said to type in the name. Now, how do I type in the name?"

She started typing but nothing happened.

"It's not doing anything in the box," said Marjorie.

"I'm typing," replied Essie, hitting one key, then another in her one-finger method. Again, Fay elbowed Essie away from the board, grabbed the mouse, and clicked on the search box where, magically, a black vertical line appeared. Fay pointed at the box, and then sat back in her wheelchair.

"How does she know how to do this?" asked Marjorie.

"Just type, Essie," said Opal. Essie's right index finger went flying (well, not flying) over the keyboard. After a few starts and stops, her efforts appeared in the magic Google box. She had typed the name "Ben Jericho."

"Now what?" she asked. "Is it supposed to do something?"

"Maybe you have to click it with that mouse thing?" suggested Marjorie.

"Maybe you have to rub the mouse thing over the box thing," offered Opal.

At this point, Fay again bent over towards the keyboard and with one finger hit the "Enter" button. Suddenly, the screen filled with a list of words and paragraphs, all containing the name "Ben Jericho."

"Oh, my!" said Marjorie. "Is all of that information about Ben Jericho?"

"It goes on and on," added Opal as she glanced from the top of the computer screen to the bottom.

"There's. . ." Essie looked at the bottom of the page where blue numbers running from "1" through "7" seemed to indicate additional information about Ben Jericho. "I think there's more information about him. Look!"

"Now what do we do?" asked Marjorie. Fay, who still had her hand on the mouse, moved the device quickly over the blue text on the first entry. She clicked her index finger on the left side of the mouse. Instantly the screen changed to a newspaper article with a photograph.

"Look!" said Marjorie. "It's a story about Ben Jericho."

Essie started reading the story, which was from the sports section of a Buffalo, New York, newspaper. "The Buffalo West High School Bulldogs were led to glory last night in a squeaker over the Provincetown Panthers. Star guard Ben Jericho made the winning goal . . ."

"Wait a minute!" shouted Opal. "Look at the date! It says 2005. If Ben Jericho was a high school basketball player in 2005, I don't think he's the one we want."

"Of course not," agreed Essie. "Remember, there must be hundreds of Ben Jerichos. In the letter, our Ben Jericho said he had trouble tracking down Bob Weiderley because of the number of Bob Weiderleys that are in the United States. I imagine there are lots of Ben Jerichos too. This one is obviously not our Ben Jericho."

"How do we go back to that part that listed all those articles?" pondered Marjorie. As if in answer to her prayer, Fay reached for the mouse, moved it to an arrow in the upper-left-hand corner of the screen and clicked. The previous page appeared.

"Oh, I get it," said Opal from behind Essie. "The arrow points backwards, so she clicked it and it sent us back to where we were."

"Very clever! Good job, Fay," agreed Essie. "Now, what do we do next?"

"Fay, do that click thing on one of these other articles," said Marjorie, pointing at the second listing in blue text on the screen.

"Do we have to just keep clicking on every article until we find our Ben Jericho? What if we never find him? What if there aren't any articles about him?" asked Essie.

"Try putting some other information in that box," suggested Opal. "Those articles seemed to have been generated by that mouse device based on the information you typed into that box, Essie. Maybe if you type in more information, the mouse will find the right Ben Jericho."

"Yes," agreed Marjorie. "We know more than just his name. Write in his name, his address, his town. Write in everything we know."

"Okay," said Essie, and she quickly went to work with her one finger typing. Soon the box was filled with the more detailed information about Ben Jericho. "Okay, now I hit this button that says 'enter,' right?" She turned to Fay who had fallen asleep.

"Yes, yes," said Marjorie, nodding.

With her finger on the "enter" button, Essie felt empowered. As she pressed it, the screen immediately brought up a new list of information—although this list was much shorter. Indeed, this list had only three items.

"Why so few?" asked Marjorie.

"Because we narrowed our parameters," said Opal.

"Math again, Opal!" chided Marjorie.

"Stop it, you two!" said Essie, bent over the three entries. She saw that the second and third entries appeared to be the same. That is, although there were some differences in the title or what she was calling the title, the descriptions below were the same and both mentioned a Ben Jericho as a local marathon runner. She didn't think that would be much help. The first article, however, referred to Ben Jericho and a local business.

"Click that first one," said Marjorie, pointing at the first item. Essie moved the mouse over the blue link and clicked. The screen changed to a lengthy article dated 1998 from the business section of a community newspaper. It discussed various individuals in local businesses who had been hired or promoted. One such individual was an executive of a local company called Medilogicos, Inc., named Ben Jericho, age 42. It gave his address and listed the names of his wife and children. The information in the article was identical to that supplied in the letter. It appeared to the women that they had found their Ben Jericho.

"It's him!" said Marjorie.

"Now what do we do?" asked Opal.

"I wish we had a way to locate the original newspaper and get a copy of it. Here, I'll write down the name of the newspaper.

Maybe I can call them and see if they can send me a copy of this newspaper."

"It's over ten years old!" said Marjorie. "They probably won't be able to do that!"

"Then, I'm going to have to write it all down. You two stand guard while I start copying."

"Essie, you can't write down that entire article!" exclaimed Opal. "It must be thousands of words!"

All the shouting woke Fay from her brief nap. She glanced over at her friends who were squabbling about recording the information on the screen. Fay reached out again for the mouse, and clicked an icon in the upper left-hand corner.

"Oh, no, Fay!" screamed Marjorie. "Now it's gone!"

"I needed to write that information down," said Essie.

Fay ignored their pleas and clicked on a tiny drawing of a printer. When another screen popped up, Fay pressed "print" and instantaneously the small printer behind the monitor leaped into life and spewed out a beautiful copy of the Ben Jericho article. Essie grabbed the single sheet from the device and sat back down where she showed it to the women.

"Oh, Moses and roses!" exclaimed Essie. "Thank you, Fay!"

"Did Fay do that?" asked Marjorie.

"She must have," replied Opal.

As the three women *oohed* and *awwed* over the newly printed copy of the newspaper article, Fay closed the print screen and clicked back into Google. Then she went back to sleep.

## Chapter Fourteen

*"It's not the years in your life that count.  It's the life in your years."*
—Abraham Lincoln

Before they left the computer station, the women (with Fay's help) also discovered and printed information on the company where Ben Jericho worked—Medilogicos, Inc.  A directory entry gave the address, phone number, and general information for the medical services provider.  It appeared that Medilogicos employed over 300 individuals and that Ben Jericho was an executive director in charge of research and development.  They were also able to find Jericho's home telephone number and they discovered that his wife, Isabel, belonged to several local charitable organizations.

Essie, Marjorie, and Opal went back to Essie's apartment, leaving Fay to finish her nap in front of the computer.  Opal whispered to Fay that she would pick her up for lunch on her way back.  Fay didn't complain.  Fay was still asleep.

In Essie's living room, the three friends argued over their next step.  Marjorie wanted to call Ben Jericho immediately and ask him directly what his intentions were towards Bob Weiderley.  Opal thought a more discreet method might be to call Jericho's wife and claim to be calling from some obscure charity and see what they could find out that way.  Essie wasn't sure.  She worried that any attempt to contact Jericho or his wife might cause the scammer to speed up his plan (whatever that plan was) and poor Bob Weiderley might find himself penniless if and when he recovered from his coma.

In the end, Opal's plan won out, being the least disruptive, yet still somewhat productive, of their options.

Essie made the call.

"Hello," she said in her cheeriest, most persuasive money-collecting voice. "Is this Mrs. Jericho?"

"Yes," replied a soft female voice. "I'm Isabel Jericho."

"Mrs. Jericho," continued Essie. "This is Margaret—(she used a first name because that's what most solicitors did when they called her to get money)—from the National Heart Disease and Cancer Research Association." She figured she'd combine two awful diseases for greater emotional impact.

Marjorie scowled and Opal's chin dropped.

"Our records indicate," said Essie, knowing that the only records most of these places had was a list of phone numbers for suckers.

"I'm sorry," interrupted Isabel Jericho, "but I'm involved in so many causes right now that I simply can't get involved in any more." With that, she hung up, leaving Essie flabbergasted.

"I can't believe she hung up on me!" gasped Essie.

"She obviously recognized a scam artist when she heard one," sneered Opal.

"Maybe because she's married to one?" queried Marjorie.

"I didn't get a chance to ask her any questions about her husband," wailed Essie.

"Should we call him at work?" asked Marjorie.

"Let's try," said Essie, lifting her finger to dial Jericho's business number.

"Why don't you let me try this time, Essie?" asked Opal.

"What?" squeaked Essie. "Just because that woman hung up on me doesn't mean that I can't talk to people persuasively."

"Can I try?" asked Opal, sweetly.

"Oh, all right! Here!" She handed the receiver to Opal and rose from her armchair, allowing Opal to sit beside the phone. Opal sat down and Essie placed the written phone number on the notepad in front of her face.

"I've got it!" said Opal, pushing the paper away. She dialed the eleven digits and waited for several rings before the call was answered.

"May I speak with Mr. Jericho?" she asked, using her best administrative assistant voice. Essie and Marjorie could hear talking on the other end of the line. "Oh? When do you expect him back? Oh. Not until then. Oh, I see. I really needed to get in touch with him." More listening. "That's too bad. I just missed him? Not for several days? My goodness. Oh, dear. I really need to contact him. It's very important." Opal pushed her case assertively and Essie and Marjorie listened intently.

"No, actually, it's not business," continued Opal. Essie realized that this tactic was probably a good one. If Jericho wasn't there and wasn't due back, it wouldn't really matter what excuse Opal gave the secretary as long as she could get some useful information. "Truthfully, it's a personal situation. You see, Mr. Jericho is a relative of mine . . . . What?" There was a long pause as Opal listened, her eyes growing wide. "He is? Do you know when? Oh, yes. Well, yes. Thank you. No, no message." Opal hung up.

"What?" asked Essie. "What did she say?"

"That was Jericho's secretary. She said that he'd left town just today on . . . personal . . . business. He isn't expected back for several days. She didn't know where he'd gone but when I told her I was a relative, she became very flustered and tried to get me to leave my name. You heard it."

"Are you thinking what I'm thinking?" questioned Marjorie.

"I'm thinking that he's on his way here to see Bob," said Essie. "Is that what you're thinking?"

"It is," agreed Opal.

"Me too," said Marjorie. "And it sounds like his secretary knows what he's up to or she suspects."

"That's what I'm thinking." said Essie. "Ladies, if that Ben Jericho is on his way to Happy Haven to see Bob, things have just become critical. I don't know what to do now."

"Are you afraid he'll find out Bob's in a coma in the hospital and try to hurt him?" asked Marjorie.

"Like in the movies?" suggested Opal. "You know, how they inject an air bubble in the poor man's IV."

"We can't let it get that far," said Essie.

At that moment, the intercom crackled to life with the announcement of the first seating for lunch.

"Come on," Essie said. "Let's get Fay and go eat. We'll need all our strength if we have to confront this Jericho fellow—and for all we know—he may get here sooner than later."

The three women rolled out of Essie's front door in single file, like a determined battalion of soldiers on their way to war.

## Chapter Fifteen

*"Age is something that doesn't matter, unless you are a cheese."*
—Billie Burke

On their way to the battleground—or in this case, the mess hall—they stopped for Fay who was still seated at the computer terminal.  She was, surprisingly enough, wide awake and plunking away at the keyboard.  As the women rolled by, Opal motioned for Fay to join them.  Fay hit the print button, grabbed the output and added it to several other papers in her fist, and then unlocked the wheels on her chair and pivoted expertly to the tail end position behind Opal.  The foursome arrived first at the entrance to the dining hall.  Santos was the Maître 'D' on duty for the day and he greeted the ladies with delight.

"Miss Essie, Miss Opal, Miss Marjorie!" he exclaimed. "And, Miss Fay!  You ladies are first in line.  You must hear that we having Cornish game hens today and that there not enough for everyone to have one!"

"Yes," agreed Essie. "Santos, we'd better all get one of those little birds, or I will hold you personally responsible!"

Santos's face fell. "Miss Essie, not to worry.  I will see you get the bird!"  He smiled encouragingly.  Essie looked at him pointedly then at her friends.  Was he pulling her leg? She suspected that Santos's English was probably much better than he let on.  Oh, well.  It didn't matter.  The glass double doors opened from inside and Santos guided the women through the entrance and towards their regular table.

After they were all seated (except for Fay who remained in her wheelchair) and their vehicles parked nearby, the four friends continued their excited conversation while they waited for their fellow diners to be seated. Each quickly glanced at the menus, but Santos was right. The Cornish game hen was the best choice and all four women selected that as their entree when Santos arrived with his order pad.

"Tell Fay what happened," said Opal to Essie.

"Really, Opal," replied Essie. "I'm really not sure she understands . . . Oh, all right anyway. Fay, we called Ben Jericho's wife but she wouldn't talk to us. Then, we called his secretary and she said he'd left town on a 'personal' matter just today and wouldn't be back for several days."

"Essie thinks he's coming here," whispered Marjorie across the table to the short lady in her wheelchair.

"She doesn't know what we're talking about," said Essie, smiling warmly at Fay. Fay's eyes were wide as she turned her head from one woman to the other.

"What's she got in her hand?" asked Marjorie.

"What?" asked Essie.

"Look," said Marjorie, pointing across the table at Fay who was clutching several sheets of paper in her left fist.

"Here, Fay," said Opal, gently. "Can I see what you have there?" She reached over and took the papers—pried them actually—from Fay's hand. She straightened them and thumbed through them—three sheets in all. "My goodness. Look at this."

"What?" asked Essie.

"Fay, you were very busy at that computer, weren't you?" questioned Opal. "It looks like she was doing some investigating of her own."

"You mean more dirt on Ben Jericho?" asked Marjorie.

"No," responded Opal. "Not Jericho. Violet."

"What?" gasped Essie.

"This is all material on Violet," said Opal.

"Our director, Violet. Miss Hendrickson," clarified Marjorie.

"Let me read," said Opal with a wave of her hand. "It says here she was involved in a campus protest back in the seventies."

"Violet was a hippy?" asked Essie. "That doesn't seem like her at all."

"Looks like it," said Opal. "Here's a photo of her holding a peace sign and giving the finger to the cameraman."

"Violet?" both Essie and Marjorie said.

"Apparently. This is over thirty years ago. She was just a young teenager here. She looks a lot different with that long straggly hair and the band around her forehead. And, of course, her name is different—probably a maiden name, but it's her all right."

"I'd say," agreed Essie. "If she was involved in political protests, who knows what else she might have done . . ."

"You mean, like poison a resident who's left five million dollars to Happy Haven?" asked Marjorie.

"Exactly," said Essie.

"Ladies," said Opal, holding up her hands to quiet them. "Just because she was a rabble rouser in her youth does not mean she's a murderer—or attempting to commit a murder."

"It sure makes me more suspicious," said Marjorie.

"Me too," said Essie.

"We're getting way off track," argued Opal. "Even if, on the very off chance that Violet somehow did something to cause Bob's collapse, it's unlikely that she's going to attempt anything else while he's hospitalized. Right now, we have bigger worries. This Ben Jericho appears to be headed this way. When he gets here, what will he do? Will he show up here at Happy Haven?"

"He'll have to," said Marjorie. "He sent the letter here. He has no way of knowing that Bob is in the hospital. But as soon as he arrives and says he's looking for Bob, some staff member will direct him to the hospital—and that isn't good. What can we do if he gets to Bob in the hospital?"

"Right," agreed Essie, "we can't protect Bob from here."

"Do we really think this Jericho fellow will attempt something at the hospital? We don't have any evidence that he's trying to do anything physically harmful to Bob. All he did was write him a letter—hardly a huge lethal threat," said Opal.

Santos arrived with four lovely little hens, each garnished with creamy cheese sauce, a crab apple, cole slaw, and a potato flan.

"Ooo! Santos! How beautiful!" squealed Marjorie.

"And it smells divine," added Opal.

"I give you the bird, Miss Essie," said Santos, placing the plate before her with a polite bow.

"Lovely, Santos!" smirked Essie. Santos took his leave and the women began cutting and eating their poultry meals.

"Fay," said Essie, "I really wish I knew what was going on in that brain of yours. You obviously know something. You knew about Bob getting that letter that led to his collapse. Now, you find all this information on Violet that suggests she has secrets in her past. Why did you suspect her? Why did you go searching for information on Violet?"

Fay looked wide-eyed as Essie stared at her.

"I don't think she understands what you're saying," said Marjorie.

"She must," countered Essie.

"Essie," explained Opal. "Fay understands a lot, but in her own way. You can't force her. She'll tell us what she wants us to know in her own time. Until then, we have to be patient."

"You're right, Opal. I'm sorry for pressuring you, Fay," said Essie. She patted Fay's hand. Fay took another bite of her hen and smiled.

"I suggest," offered Opal, "that we try to find out what we can about Violet from the staff—but discreetly."

"Yes," agreed Marjorie. "Maybe someone on the staff knows something about where she was before coming here.'"

"When did she come here?" asked Opal. "I've been here eight years and she was here when I arrived."

"She was here when I got here too," added Essie, "ten years ago."

"Ten years for me too, Essie," added Marjorie. "Remember, we came the same year. I don't think we know much about Violet because she keeps herself so removed from the residents. When I saw her when Bob collapsed the other night I hardly recognized her."

"I agree. She's a mystery," said Essie. "And while we're looking into Violet's background, we must keep our eyes open for Ben Jericho. I don't suppose it's possible for one of us to station ourselves near the front desk at all times."

"We wouldn't need to be there at night, because they lock the main door at nine," noted Marjorie.

"That's right," said Essie. "I know. Phyllis is at the desk most of the day. After five, there's usually one of the aides there. Maybe we can cue Phyllis that we're expecting this Ben Jericho and we need her to let us know when he gets here."

"But what are we going to tell her?" asked Marjorie. "We have no connection to him."

"I know," said Opal. "We can tell her that Jericho has been trying to scam one of us and we need to know as soon as he shows up!"

"That's a great idea! And it's close to the truth!" said Essie, "except that he's trying to scam Bob not us! Do you think Phyllis will go for it?"

"I don't see why not," said Marjorie.

"All we can do is try. The most important thing is that we don't let Jericho get to Bob," said Essie. "Let's see if we can find Phyllis right after lunch."

## Chapter Sixteen

*"In dog years, I'm dead."*
—Author Unknown

The friends laid out their story for Phyllis, the front desk clerk, immediately after their meal.  All bunched up at the counter, with Fay in her chair and hanging on the edge of the counter trying to see over, the women described Ben Jericho and his nefarious plot to Happy Haven's sweet counter lady.

"He tried to get me to write him a check," said Essie, "from my bank account.  If it hadn't been for my financial advisor I would have given that man most of my savings and I'd never see it again!"

The ladies nodded and made sounds of woe in the appropriate spots during Essie's heart-rending story.  Phyllis listened courteously as she always did when one of the residents had a problem.  When Essie was finished Phyllis spoke.

"Essie," she said, "this is really a serious problem.  You really need to talk to Violet about it.  We absolutely don't want this man coming here and trying to bilk our residents out of their money."

"Uh, no," replied Essie, gulping.  "I'd be . . . uh, too embarrassed to talk to Violet about this.  I just don't want to run into this fellow . . ."

"And she doesn't want him to pester anyone else here either!" added Opal.

"Essie will be fine, Phyllis," said Marjorie, "but she's really just concerned about everyone else here.  This man is a real scumbag and we want to keep him from harming any of our friends."

"Of course," replied Phyllis. "Actually, he's probably fairly easy to roadblock. If he should show up, I'll ask who he wants and whoever he says, I'll just say that no one by that name lives here."

"That's a great idea, Phyllis," said Opal. "I'm sure that will scare him away."

"What was his name again?" asked the clerk.

"Ben Jericho," replied Essie. "Here's his photograph." She handed Phyllis the picture that Jericho had mailed to Bob.

"How did you get a picture of him, Essie?" asked Phyllis.

"I . . . uh . . . oh, he gave it to me when he first started talking to me about investments. Sort of a friendly gesture, I thought."

"At the time," added Marjorie.

"He called me and he claimed to know people I knew and he said they had invested money with him. Then he came over here one afternoon and showed me all these charts . . . I was going to write him a check, but I told him I wanted to ask my financial advisor first. Then, he seemed sort of scared and he left rather quickly," explained Essie.

"I see," said Phyllis, her large, soulful brown eyes looking at all three women sympathetically. "I'm sure I can handle this, girls. Don't let it worry you anymore. If this Ben Jericho shows up, I'll send him packing in no time. In the mean time, you really need to tell Violet about this so she can decide what, if anything, needs to be done about this man."

"We will, we will," agreed Essie, smiling. Opal and Marjorie smiled and nodded their agreement and then the foursome headed on their way.

"Now what?" asked Marjorie.

"Now, I say back to that computer to see what else we can find on Violet," said Essie. "Something tells me that what Fay found may be just the tip of the iceberg."

They rolled into the family room only to discover that both computers were in use.

"What?" exclaimed Essie. "I hardly ever see anyone at those things! Now when we need one, they're all in use. Just like public toilets!"

"So what should we do?" asked Marjorie.

"I suggest some face-to-face sleuthing," said Opal. "I'm scheduled for physical therapy this afternoon up in the rec room at three o'clock. I'll ask around among the therapists to see if any of them know anything about Violet and her background." With that, she motioned to Fay and the two women rolled over to the elevator to head up to their rooms.

"I'll go play trivia at two here in the family room. I always like doing that," said Marjorie.

"Good," answered Essie, "and, you know, my hair is looking a bit disheveled. I'm going to see if Beverly can squeeze me in for a wash and set."

"Excellent!" said Marjorie.

"We can report our findings at dinner," replied Essie. "See you!" The two pals scooted around, each heading for their own rooms and their individual assignments.

Back in her living room, Essie called the beauty shop which was actually just a short distance down the hall and off the family room. She knew the shop would be open this afternoon. If she couldn't get an appointment, she could always just walk down there and chat with Beverly, the chief beautician, and a really friendly woman. Luckily, however, Bev had just had a last-minute cancellation and she was more than happy to fit Essie in for a wash and set.

Essie made a quick pit stop before leaving. At the moment she really didn't need to pee, but once she found herself in the chair at the beauty shop, she knew her opportunity to relieve herself would be sorely limited, so she took precautionary measures. Then she was off. In just a few moments, she entered the Happy Haven Beauty Shop. There was one sink and three stations with mirrors and chairs. Two chairs, of course, were unnecessary because Bev was the sole beautician. Two residents were already ensconced in plastic covers in the end chairs. Bev was winding permanent rods in the hair of Dolores Morales at the far end. A woman whom Essie didn't know was in the nearest chair.

"Essie!" called out Bev, a cigarette dangling from her lips. "Center chair! Are you in luck? Yvette O'Connor just cancelled! Say 'hi,' Bruno!"

Essie rolled over to a basket just inside the front door of the small shop and tousled the ears of Bruno, Bev's lazy but friendly sheepdog. Bev typically worked out of her home, but three afternoons a week, she opened up the Happy Haven Beauty Shop and did a roaring good business. The female residents of Happy Haven were obsessive about having their hair done regularly. Bruno always came with Bev because all of the Happy Haven residents enjoyed his company. Essie grabbed a plastic cover from a hat tree near the wall near Bruno's basket, tied it around her neck, and scooted over to the center beauty chair. She climbed in.

"That's okay, honey! Just leave your walker!" shouted Bev, cigarette still clenched between her lips. "I'll move it in a minute." Bev put the final curler in Dolores Morales' hair and tied a plastic scarf neatly around her head. Then she assisted Dolores in climbing down from the movable chair and underneath the only hair dryer at the back of the shop. She flipped the switch and handed Dolores several magazines. Then stubbing out her cigarette in an ashtray on the station behind Essie, she twirled Essie around.

"Now, doll, what are we going to do with you today?" She ran her fingers through Essie's silky white curls. "My God, I hope I have hair like yours when I'm your age!"

"You won't want to be my age!"

"What?" teased Bev, "you mean twenty-two?"

"Ninety!" said Essie with a combination of pride and horror.

"That's impressive, Essie!" said Bev. She got out her equipment in preparation for the haircut.

"Just the regular, Bev," said Essie, leaning back and glancing over at the other woman in the chair next to hers. This woman had a head full of curlers and was reading a magazine. "Hi," she said to the stranger. "I'm Essie. I'm on the first floor—C103."

"Stella Grainger," replied the woman, reaching out from under her long plastic cape and shaking Essie's hand. "Second floor—D144."

"Nice to meet you."

"Nice to meet you too. I just moved in a week ago."

"Okay, ladies," interrupted Bev, "have to break this up. Essie come on, let's get you washed." She helped Essie down and over to the sink where she seated her, leaned her back, and then expertly wet and washed her hair with a spray nozzle.

"It's always nice to meet new residents," said Essie. "But it reminds me of how long I've been here."

"How long is that, Essie?" asked Bev as she wrapped a towel around her head and directed her back to the middle chair.

"Ten years," replied Essie. "Doesn't seem that long."

"Nope," agreed Bev, running a large, thick-toothed comb through Essie's curls. "Bruno and I've been coming here even longer than that. Let's see. Going on fifteen years; right, Bruno?"

Bruno barked once in agreement.

"Wow!" said Essie. "You know everybody here then."

"I know pretty much everybody who's here and everybody who was here. If you know what I mean," said Bev, laughing.

"Did you know the person who was the Director before Violet Hendrickson?" asked Essie.

"Hmmm," said Bev, thinking to herself, "let's see. That Violet's been here a long time. But, no, if I remember correctly there was some guy here before her. Can't remember his name. I think Violet arrived maybe some few years after I started coming here."

"Do you know why her predecessor left?" asked Essie. "Or why they hired Violet?"

"Heck," said Bev, "I don't pay much attention to that kind of stuff. As long as they let me keep my beauty parlor and let me open it on the days that are convenient to me, nothing else really matters. You know, I do remember some weird stuff going on back then."

"Like what?" asked Essie.

"It's so long ago," said Bev. "I think there might have been some flack about hiring Violet. I think one of the members of the Board was opposed or something, but I guess in the final count, the Board approved her because—well—she's here and she's been here for almost as long as I've been here."

"What was the Board member worried about?"

"Gee, Essie," said Bev, contorting her face, obviously trying to remember. "I can't remember anything specific. It all blew over anyway. I think one of the Board members was very supportive of her and may have convinced the other Board member that she was the right person for the position."

"Do you think she's a good Director, Bev?" asked Essie.

"I don't know," said Bev. "Personally, I have no real interaction with the woman. I will admit though that I do hear some residents talk about her from time to time in here. Sometimes, what they say isn't very flattering."

"Such as?"

"Oh, you know," said Bev, with a shrug, "she's a tough bird. She's a drill sergeant."

"And the staff?"

"Probably more complaints from them," said Bev, under her breath. "With the exception of the Social Director, that Sue Barber."

"You mean, Sue doesn't complain about Violet as much as the other staff members."

"I mean Sue Barber doesn't complain about her at all. In fact, she's usually singing her praises. Seems a little strange given that most of the rest of the staff are not that complimentary about Violet."

By this point, Bev had managed to whip about a dozen pink foam rollers into Essie's hair.

"Ready for the dryer!" she announced. Leading Essie down from the chair, she had her exchange places with Dolores who apparently was now dry. She placed Essie under the dryer and hit the button. Immediately, all Essie could hear was the blasting of hot air. She hoped that Bev wasn't producing other wonderful tidbits of information about the nefarious Violet Hendrickson. She looked over and noticed that Bev had removed the rollers from Stella Grainger's hair and had combed out her chin-length, grayish-blonde hair into a flattering style that made her new friend Stella look like she had stepped out of the pages of *Vogue*. *She's much too glamorous for Happy Haven*, thought Essie. *Oh well, she's new. Give her a few years here and she'll become frumpy just like me. Oh, stop it, Essie!* She scolded herself for such self-pity. She had a mystery to solve and she had to get back to work.

After Bev finished the comb-out on Stella Grainger, she took Stella's payment, handed her a receipt, and the new resident of Happy Haven left the shop with a friendly wave to her new buddies. Bev then turned her attention to Dolores Morales, removing her rollers and styling Dolores' thick, pitch black hair in a way that brought out Dolores' magenta-colored eyes. *Bev is truly a miracle worker*, thought Essie. After she finished with Dolores, and she and Bev were alone in the shop, Bev brought Essie back to her chair, removed her rollers, and fluffed out her hair.

"Such gorgeous curls!" she sighed. "You must have all the gentlemen swooning."

"Hardly," laughed Essie. "My swoon-producing days are over."

"Now, Essie," said Bev, "you're never too old for romance. My goodness, there are couples here older than you!"

"Really, who?" asked Essie, incredulous.

Bev bent close to Essie's ear and whispered, "Jasper Pettridge and Molly McMasters."

"No!" cried Essie. "He must be 86 if he's a day!"

"I know," agreed Bev, "and that Clarence Bellows is always flirting with little Emily Simpson and her friend Gertrude Jeter. And you know, Bob Weiderley was wining and dining Evelyn Cudahy—before he got sick."

"What?"

"I saw them together all the time. I think they used to meet in the chapel. I believe she's been getting chemotherapy for breast cancer," added Bev.

"You mean Bob and Evelyn were more than just—friends?" asked Essie.

"Of course, I can't prove anything, but I'd see them get on the elevator together. He's on the second floor and I believe she's on the first floor, isn't she?"

"I don't know," replied Essie, now totally befuddled.

"Anyway," continued Bev, putting the finishing touches on Essie's do, "if there was hanky-panky going on, it might explain why he collapsed. I mean, all that—activity—can be hard on an old guy's heart."

"I guess it can. Thanks, Bev. I mean, thanks for doing my hair at the last minute."

"No problem, sweetie!" chirped Bev and, giving Essie a hug, she helped her down from the chair. "Don't forget to say good-bye to Bruno."

Essie grabbed her walker and rolled over to the big sleeping dog. She patted his head gently and then turned and headed out of the shop and back to her room. She had a lot to think about.

# Chapter Seventeen

*"I don't know how you feel about old age . . . but in my case I didn't even see it coming. It hit me from the rear."*
—Phyllis Diller

Essie pushed her walker slowly into the family room. She was lost in thought as she contemplated the few pieces of juicy gossip—or she hoped, genuine information—that Bev had supplied her. Violet got the Director position at Happy Haven after an apparent disagreement among several Board members. She wondered which Board members were involved and if they were still on the Board today. Violet obviously had a champion on the Board. Who was it and why?

Then there was the totally unexpected news that Bob Weiderley and Evelyn Cudahy were an item. Of course, Bev could be wrong. Evelyn could have been seen getting in the elevator with Bob for some totally innocent reason. After all, the woman was seriously ill. It hardly seemed likely that she'd be having some torrid affair (or as torrid as anyone could have at age 86) with sweet Bob Weiderley. *Stranger things,* Essie reminded herself.

As she glanced up towards the front desk, she noticed a man standing there talking to Phyllis. He was wearing a well-tailored brown suit. At first, she thought he was probably just one of numerous salesmen that made the rounds, trying to sell some new geriatric service or product to Violet (who was the person who dealt with these individuals, and usually, so she heard, rather curtly). However, as she looked at the man and moved her walker a bit closer so she could get a better look at his face, she realized that he was not a salesperson, but Ben Jericho. She thought she recognized him from the photograph he'd included in the envelope.

Quickly, Essie plopped down on the nearest armchair and reached into the compartment under her walker's seat and brought out the envelope she'd stolen—or rather borrowed—from Bob Weiderley's apartment. She opened it and surreptitiously removed the photograph of Ben Jericho.

Bringing the picture close to her eyes and then peeking over the top at the man at the counter—then back again at the photograph—then back again to the man at the counter, Essie realized that it was the man that she and Marjorie and Opal had been discussing ever since finding the infamous letter. Ben Jericho, scam artist! There he was trying to bamboozle poor Phyllis. *Oh, leaping Lucifer*! She hoped that Phyllis remembered to divert his attention and not let him know where Bob was—or even that Bob was a resident at Happy Haven.

As Essie watched from the safety of her chair in the family room, the discussion between Phyllis and Ben Jericho appeared to be getting more heated. The man was waving a paper in front of Phyllis and pointing to something on it. Phyllis was smiling politely but shrugging. *Go, Phyllis*! said Essie silently to the front desk clerk. Finally, the man heaved his shoulders, turned, and headed out the front entrance.

Quickly, Essie rose and guided her walker over to the front desk.

"Phyllis," she whispered to the clerk, who had turned back to return to the room behind her desk.

"Oh, Essie," said Phyllis, returning to the counter. "You'll never believe it. That man—that scam artist you warned me about—he was just here—looking for Bob Weiderley!"

"Yes," said Essie, "I saw him! Goodness gratefulness, Phyllis, you handled him well! He seemed really mad!"

"He was," agreed Phyllis, "and he really wanted to see Bob. He told me his name was Jericho like you said and he said he knew Bob was a resident here. I gave him the runaround and said a person had to be on an approved visitor list before we could let them in to see a resident."

"You didn't tell him that Bob was in the hospital, did you?" asked Essie.

"Oh, no!" she exclaimed, clutching the lapels of her pink work jacket together. "I would never do that! But, Essie, I really have to tell Violet about this. It was one thing when this Jericho's arrival was a possibility, but now that he's actually shown up, Violet has to be told. This could escalate, possibly into something very dangerous for Bob or some of our other residents."

Essie clutched the handles of her walker as she thought about the wisdom of revealing any information to Phyllis about the letter, Ben Jericho, and his possible relationship to Bob. Was it best to fill her in on the truth? Or should she maintain her cover story? If Phyllis told Violet about her confrontation with Ben Jericho, things could quickly get out of hand. Of course, no one had to know about the letter, she realized. She could just return it to Bob's apartment and no one would be the wiser (except for herself, Opal, Marjorie, and Fay). Maybe it would be better in the long run for Violet to be warned about Ben Jericho so she could protect Bob and the other residents if—probably when—he returned.

In the end, she decided to keep quiet about the letter and let Phyllis tell Violet about Jericho's recent appearance. If necessary, she could return the letter. If she told Phyllis about the letter, then she'd have to explain how she got the letter and then Violet would no doubt be told that Essie Cobb was a thief. Not a reputation she wanted to cultivate at Happy Haven. She'd probably lose any friends she had because they'd worry that she'd break into their apartments the minute their backs were turned.

"Yes," said Essie to the clerk. "You'd probably better tell Violet about this Jericho fellow. Then she can keep an eye out for him and handle him herself if he shows up again."

"Oh, he'll show up again," said Phyllis, her short pony tail swinging in punctuation as she spoke, "he made that very clear when he left. And my guess is that it won't be long. I'm going to call for Violet now." She moved over to the intercom system against the wall.

"I'd better get going," said Essie as she turned her walker.

"Oh, no, Essie!" cried Phyllis from the intercom. "Wait here! I'm sure Violet will want to ask you about this man. You're the one who knows the most about him."

*Yikes and dikes*, thought Essie. *Just what I need.* Essie could hear Violet's voice responding to Phyllis's call on the intercom. She said she would be right there.

Essie twitched nervously as she stood by the front counter. She hoped that Mother Nature didn't send her a call just now because she needed to be able to concentrate on dealing with Violet—not on her bladder. Almost at once, Violet, wearing a striking black suit with a red silk blouse and sling back leather heels, appeared from the office wing off the side of the dining hall. She walked purposefully to the front desk towards Phyllis, ignoring Essie who was standing there watching her arrival.

"What is this, Phyllis?" asked the Director of Happy Haven, pen tapping on the counter.

"Miss Violet," said Phyllis, "a man was just here demanding to visit Bob Weiderley."

"I assume you told him that Mr. Weiderley is in the hospital?" asked Violet, head tipped expectantly.

"Uh, no," continued Phyllis, "I didn't. You see, Essie here . . ." She motioned towards Essie standing beside Violet. "had warned me the other day that this same man—his name is Ben Jericho—had tried to scam her out of some money. Essie was worried that he'd be back here to try the same ploy on other residents. When he showed up asking to see Bob Weiderley, I—uh—I was worried that he intended to do the same thing to Bob, so I made up something."

"What did you make up, Phyllis?" asked Violet Hendrickson, scowling and tapping the toe of her elegant heel.

"I—uh, said he wasn't on an approved visitors' list, so I couldn't let him in," replied the clerk.

Violet scratched her ear and tucked her shiny black hair behind it. She took several intentionally deep breaths.

"I wish you'd called me," she said to Phyllis. "Now, where is this man?"

"He left, Miss Violet," said Phyllis, "but he was mad. I really think he'll be back."

"When he does come back, contact me right away," said a curt Violet Hendrickson. Then, she turned abruptly on her high heels and walked at a fast clip out of the lobby.

"Wowsy dowsy!" whispered Essie to Phyllis when Violet had disappeared into her office. "What does that mean?"

"Who knows?" said Phyllis. "But it's out of our hands, Essie. I have to report to Violet if this Jericho guy shows up again."

"Sure," agreed Essie, nodding. "I understand." She didn't understand. She actually had no idea what Violet intended to do if and when Ben Jericho returned. Would he be able to sweet talk Violet? Or would Violet let him have it with both barrels as she was capable of doing—and as Essie had just seen her do? Yes, Violet was cultured and sophisticated, but it was clear that Phyllis had been scolded and knew it. And Essie was the reason for the scolding. She felt really bad for Phyllis—she was only trying to help. Essie turned tail and, after waving farewell to the desk clerk, headed back to her room.

## Chapter Eighteen

*"The best thing about getting older is that you don't lose all the other ages you've been."*
---Madeleine L'Engle

She had barely entered her apartment when the phone rang. Essie sighed, rolled over to her chair, and lowered herself into the cushion, and then reached over for her telephone.

"Hello," she announced into the receiver.

"Essie," said a voice at the other end, "this is Phyllis at the front desk. You need to come back to the lobby right away. Bye." Then the frazzled-sounding clerk hung up. Essie sat there in her comfortable chair, longing to remain there for at least a brief while. Instead, she got up, zipped as quickly as she could into her bathroom for a quick emptying and then as fast as her thin legs were capable, she rolled out again and back to the front counter.

As she got closer, she saw not only Phyllis behind the counter, but Violet also there holding a folder and looking grim. Beside her, Ben Jericho stood, arms folded. As Violet and Phyllis watched Essie's arrival, Ben Jericho also looked in her direction. Essie moved closer, hesitantly, three sets of eyes glaring at her.

"Let's sit down," said Violet Hendrickson to Ben Jericho and Essie, motioning the two of them to the arm chairs arranged in a square directly in front of the desk. Phyllis remained at the front desk, smiling. It was obvious that Violet no longer had need of her input. Violet positioned herself between Essie and Ben Jericho, sitting on the very edge of a paisley hard back cane chair. Essie slouched into the softest armchair in the grouping. Jericho chose the end of a rose velvet sofa. Violet held her folder like a sword, tapping it against her other palm menacingly. "Now," began

Violet, nodding from Jericho to Essie. "Let's get to the bottom of this. Mr. Jericho, you tell me that you are here to visit Bob Weiderley."

"Yes, I was here earlier," said Jericho, "but your desk clerk told me I couldn't see him because I wasn't on an approved visitors' list."

"Umm," noted Violet, neither agreeing nor disagreeing. "And your reason for visiting Mr. Weiderley?"

"Is personal," responded Jericho succinctly.

"Hummph!" snorted Essie to the man.

"Who is this woman?" demanded Jericho.

Violet held up her palm to the visitor.

"Essie," she said, turning to her, "you told us that this man attempted to scam you out of a lot of money recently."

"What?" shouted Jericho.

"I . . . I . . .—" sputtered Essie.

"Did this man attempt to take your money, Essie?" asked Violet, looking unwaveringly into Essie's eyes. Essie withdrew her eyes from Violet's glare and peered at the face of Ben Jericho. Of course, she recognized the man as the face in the photograph inside the envelope that now was hidden in the compartment in her walker, but she obviously couldn't reveal that.

"Essie?" pressed Violet.

"Actually . . .—" squeaked Essie in a tiny voice, "now that I look at him, I don't think it's the same man."

"But, Essie, you said the man who scammed you was named Ben Jericho."

"Uh, did I?" she waffled. "Maybe I just mentioned to Phyllis that this man looked like that scammer and Phyllis happened to say his name and maybe I happened to think that name sounded like the name of the man who scammed me . . . . I'm not really positive, Miss Violet." She gave Violet a wistful look, trying to appear as absentminded and senile as she definitely wasn't.

"Oh," said Violet, continuing to tap her folder on her palm. "Mr. Jericho, I believe we may owe you an apology. We're truly sorry. Sometimes a resident gets a—bee in her bonnet." At this point she turned her head and glared at Essie. "Sometimes a resident comes to believe something that simply isn't true and is able to convince our staff." She turned her head around and raised her voice loud enough so that Phyllis standing behind the counter realized that she was being included in this group chastisement.

Ben Jericho appeared flustered and mystified by this little drama that only peripherally appeared to pertain to him.

"That's all right," said the man, "I understand. I had elderly parents and sometimes . . .—" He let his argument trail as he became lost in a memory. Essie watched the man's face.

"Wonderful," said Violet, beaming as soon as she had received what she obviously considered the appropriate response—that is, a response that would not get Happy Haven—or her—in any difficulty, particularly any legal difficulty. "Now that we have that misunderstanding cleared up, how can I help you, Mr. Jericho? Just what are you trying to sell to Mr. Weiderley?"

"I'm not trying to sell him anything," said Jericho, his face falling in surprise. "It's a personal matter. I sent him a letter and I was hoping I'd hear back from him. When I didn't, I called but got no answer. So finally, I decided I'd just drive down here and try to talk to him myself."

"I see," said Violet, still tapping. She chewed her lower lip. Essie could see her dilemma. Should she—could she—ethically reveal to this man Bob's whereabouts considering she didn't know him and didn't know whether or not Bob would want him to be made aware of his location? Even if he wasn't a scam artist, Violet was ethically bound to protect Bob Weiderley and as Bob was presently in a coma there was no way for her to ask Bob whether or not he wanted this Ben Jericho to know where he was.

"Really, Miss . . . uh . . . Hendrickson," continued Jericho, "I only wish to speak briefly with Mr. Weiderley. I'd be happy to talk to him here in the lobby—in your presence, if that will make you feel better. If you believe I pose some sort of threat to him, you can search me or whatever you need to do. You can run a background check. I assure you, my intentions towards Mr. Weiderley are honorable and I mean him no harm."

"Actually," stated Violet, "that won't be possible." Essie waited with baited breath to see how Violet would handle Jericho's request.

"What?" cried out Jericho. "Just a brief conversation?"

"Mr. Jericho," she said calmly, "it's not that we wish to prevent you from conversing with Mr. Weiderley. It's simply that he's not here at the moment."

"I can wait," replied Jericho.

"You might have to wait quite some time," said Violet.

Essie cringed, fearing that the Director was going to tell the man that the person he sought was two blocks down the road in the Fairview Hospital. However, she didn't.

"No," said Violet, smiling warmly at the man, "Mr. Weiderley is on vacation with several of his buddies."

"But he must be 85 or 86," noted Jericho.

"Yes," agreed Violet, "but he's very vital. Every year about this time, a group of his old Army buddies get together for a fishing trip. I'm not really certain where they've gone or exactly when they'll return."

"You'd let him leave just like that?" queried Jericho.

"Sir," said Violet, now standing to indicate that she considered the meeting finished, "this is not a prison. Our residents are free to leave when they wish. All we ask is that they sign out. Mr. Weiderley signed out several days ago with a return date listed as 'unknown' and a destination listed as 'fishing.'" She opened her folder and appeared to be reading from Bob's file.

Jericho sighed audibly and shook his head. "Can I leave my number? I'd appreciate if you'd call if you hear from him before he returns."

"Absolutely," responded Violet, accepting the business card from the man. "Have a nice day." With a nod, she stepped quickly out of the lobby and back into the office wing. Jericho remained standing before the chair. Essie looked up at him.

"Mr. Jericho," she said, "I really am sorry I caused you this trouble. You really want to contact Bob, don't you?"

"You'll never know," sighed Jericho, sliding back down into the chair. Essie leaned forward and spoke warmly to him.

"I really did think you were that scam artist at first," she confided, "but now that I've met you, I can see that you are genuine. You do just want to talk to Bob, don't you?"

"Do you know where he went fishing, Miss . . . Essie?" asked Jericho, reaching out and grabbing one of her hands in his.

"Are you visiting here for long, Mr. Jericho?" she asked.

"I just got here this morning. I checked into a motel nearby because I planned to spend some time . . . uh . . . talking to Bob, Mr. Weiderley."

"Sometimes Bob contacts one of his friends here at Happy Haven when he's . . . on one of his . . . fishing trips."

"You mean you, Miss Essie?" he asked.

"Oh, no!" she laughed. "I'm not at his table." Jericho looked puzzled. Essie continued. "Everyone is assigned to a table and we eat all our meals at the same table. So we really get to know our tablemates."

"I see," he replied. "Do you know Mr. Weiderley's tablemates?"

She thought about revealing this information, which of course, she knew, but hesitated because she assumed that Jericho would immediately contact Hazel, Rose, or Evelyn and none of them would have a second thought about telling him Bob's whereabouts. "Uh, no, I don't know them. Actually, I don't know Mr. Weiderley all that well. I believe I played cards with him once or twice."

"Did you like him?" he asked.

"Very much," she said. "A very sweet, gentle man. I'd hate for anything bad to happen to him."

"I wouldn't want anything . . . bad . . . to happen to him either. So, he plays cards and likes to go fishing?" he asked her.

"What?" she said, confused. "Oh, yes fishing." Of course, as far as she knew, Bob Weiderley had never been fishing a day in his life.

"My Dad used to take me fishing," said Ben Jericho wistfully.

"I'm sure that's a wonderful way for a father and a son to bond," she replied as he continued to reminisce.

"A father and son. Yes," he said.

"Do you live far from here, Mr. Jericho?" she asked.

"About two hundred miles," he said, "not too far to drive, but not a trip I can make every day."

"You're a busy man?"

"Yes, unfortunately," he answered, "but I cleared a few days to come down here."

"This trip must be very important to you, then," she suggested.

"It's the most important thing in my life," he said seriously, looking at his hands.

"What hotel are you in, Mr. Jericho?" she asked at length.

"The Magnolia Hotel," he replied, "it's just a few miles down this street. Here, Miss Essie, let me give you my card. If you should hear from Mr. Weiderley or if you think of any way I can contact him, would you please call me? I have a cell phone and this bottom number is my direct personal line." He handed her an embossed card with black and gold filigreed lettering noting the name of the company—Medilogicos—and underneath his name—several phone numbers and an email address.

"Of course, Mr. Jericho," she said, taking the card and examining it. "This is a beautiful business card. What does your company do?"

"We produce computer software for various medical devices and services. Actually, we are one of the few companies in the world that is devoted to such services."

"My, my!" she replied. "How impressive! And it says here you're the Executive Director of Research and Development."

"That's just business lingo," he replied modestly. "It should just say 'inventor.'"

"Your family must be very proud of you."

"Proud, I don't know," he said laughing. "My wife would probably just like to see more of me. My kids think I'm a geek."

She laughed and he joined her. Finally, he rose and bent down and gave her a brief hug and then turned and exited the front entrance.

Essie followed him with her eyes and then looked back down at his business card, gleaming in her hands.

## Chapter Nineteen

*"Old wood best to burn, old wine to drink, old friends to trust, and old authors to read."*
—Francis Bacon

When she arrived back in her apartment, the telephone was ringing again. *Oh no*, she thought. *Not again*! However, when she answered, it was only her oldest daughter Prudence confirming her doctor appointment for the next morning. Prudence typically took her to all of her appointments and tomorrow's outing was quite a distance—to a neighboring town where her gerontologist (a fancy term for old people's doctor) had her office. Luckily, Essie only had to see this particular doctor twice a year. Essie considered the long trip a complete waste of time. The lady physician usually just asked her a few inane questions, renewed her prescription, and then sent her on her way. The only good thing about the outings was that she and Pru could enjoy all the wonderful flowering trees that lay between Happy Haven and the doctor's faraway location.

Essie was exhausted—even more than usual. That encounter with Ben Jericho and the confrontation she was forced to endure with Violet had taken the stuffing out of her—as her father would have said. After a quick potty break, she rolled over to her bed and fell backwards onto her soft mattress. She was sound asleep in a few minutes. When she woke up—seemingly just a little bit later—she was refreshed. Glancing at her wristwatch, she realized that it was almost time for dinner. In fact, she expected the dinner call to come over the intercom at any moment. She pulled herself up. Her bones ached. She had been scooting around much too fast and much too far in the last day or two in her efforts to track down the cause of Bob Weiderley's collapse at Bingo. She really needed to take it easy. And she would, she promised herself, just after she figured out what had happened to Bob and what she could do to help him.

Pulling herself upright and hanging onto her walker for support, she pushed herself into her bathroom and ran a brush through her newly coifed hair. How quickly a new style became disheveled! She looked like a chicken, feathers jutting out everywhere from her scalp. *Oh, well*, she shrugged, patting her nose with a small powder puff. *That's good enough for now*. Grabbing the rubber handles on her walker, she headed out her apartment door just as the Intercom sizzled to life and Phyllis's sweet voice sang out the call to dinner.

She was first at the entrance; the waiter in charge let her through and she wheeled herself to her table. Another waiter came around and poured her water and asked if she'd like anything to drink. She ordered iced tea and opened her menu and began to read the evening's choices while she waited for Marjorie, Opal, and Fay to arrive. Soon more residents began to fill the hall. Eventually, her three table companions arrived, talking and laughing as they took their places. Waiters soon surrounded the table again and brought the newcomers their chosen drinks.

"I suppose I should call our meeting to order," said Essie when the waiters had receded and the women were alone. "I have a lot to report. How about the rest of you?"

"Not much," answered Marjorie, "because the lady who ran the trivia game today was brand new—a volunteer. It was her first time. I doubt she even knew the names of the players at the table, let alone any dirt on anyone else. Sorry."

"What about the players?" asked Essie. "Did you get a chance to talk to any of them?"

"The only one that might be of interest to us was Hazel Brubaker," said Marjorie. "I did sort of indicate to her my concern for Bob and she seemed thankful for it. He appears to be still in a coma. She did say that Rose was visiting him again today with her daughter."

"That's something," said Essie. "Opal, look over at Bob's table. Is Rose there?"

"No," said Opal. "I only see two women at that table. I think just Hazel and Evelyn."

"Maybe Rose is still at the hospital," offered Marjorie.

"Maybe," agreed Essie. "What about you, Opal? Did you find out anything at physical therapy?"

"Not about Bob," noted tall, stern Opal, stretching out her arms, "but I did learn a few pieces of interesting information about some of the staff members."

"Do tell," said Marjorie, leaning over the table.

"You know the therapists come in from the outside. They're not employed by Happy Haven directly. So, I'm guessing that the reason they talk among themselves about staff members here is probably because they know that no one here has any authority over them."

"Probably," agreed Essie.

"Anyway," continued Opal, "one of the therapists who evidently has been working with patients here for many years was complaining about some of the procedures here. You know, how workers sometimes talk as if their clients either aren't listening or don't care about what they're saying. Anyway, one therapist was complaining about Violet and her strict requirements for the therapists. The therapist was saying that she worked for this particular therapy service—not for Violet. She took her orders from this service, but Violet gave orders to her and expected her to obey them as if Violet had the authority to fire a therapist if she wanted."

"Couldn't Violet refuse to let a therapist work on a resident if she didn't like the therapist?" asked Marjorie.

"I doubt it, unless the therapist did something so egregious that it became a matter of safety or legality," countered Opal. "So, another therapist agreed with this first therapist and they went back and forth for a good twenty minutes complaining about Violet and what a dictator she was."

"I don't know if that helps us," mused Essie. "We already knew Violet was strict and that the employees didn't really like her."

"That's what I found out," said Opal with a shrug. "Take it or leave it." She turned her nose up slightly and inhaled deeply.

"What did you find out, Essie?" asked Marjorie. With a gleam in her eye, Essie proceeded to regale her tablemates with the new found knowledge that she had gleaned about Violet and the Board of Directors from Bev the beautician.

"I bet Fay can find out more about Violet and the Board of Directors and how she got her job," suggested Opal. "What about it, Fay?"

Fay, who was starting to drift off, quickly perked up when she heard her name called.

"Fay, can you put those computer skills of yours to use and find out how Violet got her job here? Seems there was a battle among the members of the Board of Directors about her," said Essie.

Fay smiled at Essie and then nodded slowly up and down, her eyes turning back to the kitchen.

"Does she understand?" Essie asked Opal and Marjorie.

"Who knows?" said Opal. "Just let the information sink in. Then just watch and wait. If she's going to do something, she'll do it."

"Great," noted Essie. "I hope she does something quickly."

"Be patient, Essie," said Marjorie calmly. "It's not like we have to rush to meet a deadline."

"You mean like if that Ben Jericho should arrive on the scene," suggested Essie.

"Right," said Opal. "At least that hasn't happened."

"But it has!" said Essie. "He arrived this afternoon! I saw him at the front desk!"

"Oh dear," shrieked Marjorie. "What did you do?"

"I watched as Phyllis managed to talk him into leaving," she said.

"Marvelous!" cried Opal. "That Phyllis is fantastic!"

"Not so fast," said Essie, holding up her palms. "The man returned shortly afterwards and demanded to see the Director."

"Violet!" cried Marjorie.

"The one and only," said Essie. "I had barely returned to my room, thinking I was safe when Phyllis called and told me Violet wanted me in the lobby immediately."

"Ooops!" said Marjorie, with a grimace.

Essie related to her friends the events that followed the confrontation between Violet, Ben Jericho, and herself. She also informed them that after talking to Jericho face-to-face she had changed her opinion of him and now believed that he was genuine and truly was trying to track down his biological father. "Although he didn't tell me that," she added. "Of course, I didn't tell him where Bob was either—or even hint that I knew where he was. I think that's just being cautious. And, of course, it's none of my business. It's totally up to Bob whether or not he wants to meet this Ben Jericho."

"If he comes out of the coma," suggested Opal.

"When," Marjorie added firmly.

"So, Essie," said Opal, "what's our next step?"

"More investigation," replied Essie. "Fay will look into the situation with Violet and the Board of Directors—and if she doesn't, we can try to find out ourselves on that computer. I will try to find out how Bob is doing . . ."

"Essie, look!" Marjorie whispered, pulling on Essie's sleeve. "Rose Lane just arrived at her table. She must have returned from visiting Bob at the hospital. She's talking to Evelyn now. Hazel is listening, but Evelyn is clasping Rose's hands."

"Oh, my," said Essie, glancing around so she could see the scene taking place at Bob Weiderley's table. As Rose spoke to Evelyn, all three women could see a dramatic difference in the faces of Evelyn and Hazel, even from this distance. Both were now smiling broadly. Evelyn stood and hugged Rose tightly. Then all three women sat back down. "That looks like good news, wouldn't you say?"

"I would," said Opal, nodding. "Very good news."

Suddenly the intercom sputtered to life, and Phyllis's voice reverberated through the dining hall.

"Residents, I am happy to report that we have just received word that Bob Weiderley has come out of his coma. Doctors are cautiously optimistic about his recovery."

At the announcement, a cheer arose throughout the dining hall followed by applause. Everyone looked over at Bob's table and waved to Bob's tablemates who in turn nodded and waved back to their friends around the room.

"This is fantastic news," said Essie. "Once Bob returns, he'll be able to deal with this Ben Jericho and we can bow out of the picture."

"He may wonder where the letter is," suggested Marjorie, "as he left it on his desk."

"Yes," said Essie, "I agree. We're going to have to return that letter before Bob comes home."

"We?" cried Opal.

"We broke into his apartment together," argued Essie, "so we should break in together and return the letter."

"Why don't you just put it in his mailbox?" offered Marjorie.

"Bob's not stupid!" countered Essie. "He knows where he left the letter—and it wasn't in his mailbox."

"I know," suggested Opal, "just give the letter to one of the cleaning ladies. Tell her you found it on the floor and you don't know where it belongs. She'll see Bob's name and she'll probably put it in his apartment."

"I can't trust that anyone would do that," said Essie. "A cleaning lady might just give the letter to Violet and she might see that it's open and read it! No, we have to return it ourselves."

Oh, all right, Essie," said Marjorie. "I'll help you."

"I will too," Opal agreed begrudgingly.

"Let's do it right after dinner," said Essie. "There's some piano player performing tonight so most residents will be in the lobby listening and the hallways should be fairly deserted."

"We can leave Fay at the computer," suggested Opal. "Maybe she'll find something about Violet while we're breaking and entering."

"You'll have to get the security lock key again," said Essie to Opal.

"I know," said Opal, "and I can snag it if you and Marjorie will distract Phyllis for a minute or two."

"Done!" chirped Marjorie.

"Let's go!" said Marjorie, "I'd like to finish my burgling early so I can come listen to Liberace or whoever is playing."

## Chapter Twenty

*"What most persons consider as virtue, after the age of 40 is simply a loss of energy."*
—Voltaire

After again swiping the security lock key from the small basket on Phyllis's desk, Opal joined Essie and Marjorie. The three women parked Fay in front of one of the computer terminals in the family room and then took the elevator back to Bob's apartment on the second floor.  They repeated the same routine they had used previously with Opal standing guard by the corner where the back hallway met the main hallway.  Essie and Marjorie removed the lock and slipped quietly inside Bob's apartment.  Once inside, Essie removed the envelope from under her walker seat and placed it back on Bob's desk in the same position in which she found it— she thought.

"Does this look natural, Marjorie?" she asked her friend who was standing near the door.

"Come on, Essie," whispered Marjorie, "Just drop it and let's get going."

"But I want to put it just like I found it."

"I don't remember what it looked like because you grabbed it while I was in the bedroom."

"Come here."

"Oh, for heaven's sake!"  Marjorie scooted over to the desk.  "It looks fine.  Leave it and let's go."

"Maybe more like this," said Essie, turning the blotter sideways and slipping the envelope into the side sleeves.  As she lifted up the corner of the large rectangle, Marjorie looked underneath.

"Essie, what's that?"

"What?" She set the blotter to the side of the desk and picked up an aged piece of folded newsprint.

"Open it," demanded Marjorie.

Carefully, Essie unfolded the newspaper article, revealing an old police report from the *Hartford Journal* of 1995. A short paragraph indicated the arrest and conviction of one Violet Hendrickson for DUI. An accompanying photograph showed the Violet they knew but younger and looking nowhere near as glamorous as she presently did. Marjorie read over Essie's shoulder. As soon as they had completed reading the short paragraph, the two women looked at each other.

"Violet has a criminal record," whispered Marjorie.

"And Bob knew about it," added Essie.

"That's not good," said Marjorie.

"Not if Violet knew he knew," agreed Essie. "Let's get out of here. I'm leaving both of these items." She replaced the newspaper clipping under the blotter and the envelope on top.

They quickly exited the apartment, replaced the lock, and rolled themselves down the hallway where they caught up with Opal standing guard at the juncture to the main corridor. The ladies rolled together around the corner and down the long carpeted hall. At the elevator, when the door opened, they found themselves staring directly into the faces of the three women who had become known to them as Bob's girls.

"Essie!" cried Evelyn, tonight wearing a particularly lovely purple silk scarf wrapped and tied around her head. "Did you hear about Bob?"

"Yes," replied Essie, somewhat flustered, "how wonderful! He's out of the coma, I hear!"

"Yes, how wonderful!" agreed Opal and Marjorie.

"I was there in his hospital room when he came to," said Rose, beaming and squeezing Evelyn's arm protectively. Hazel stood on the other side of Evelyn, very close to her, somewhat like a guard dog.

"How is he . . . doing?" asked Essie. "Do the doctors think he'll be coming home soon?"

"It's too soon to tell," said Rose, "but I know he wants to get back here as fast as he can." She squeezed Evelyn's arm again and smiled warmly at her friend. Hazel touched her hand to Evelyn's shoulder.

"Did you speak to him?" Marjorie asked Rose.

"Just a bit," answered Rose, "then the nurses swished us out of his room so they could run tests. It's fine with me. Just knowing he's coming back soon is all that matters, isn't that right, Evelyn?"

"Yes!" said Evelyn, who had one small tear rolling down her cheek.

Essie, Opal, and Marjorie smiled warmly at the three women and then cautiously traded places with them in the elevator. Rose and Hazel both used canes. Evelyn used nothing, but even so she seemed the frailest of the three. Essie, Opal, and Marjorie all used walkers and the small elevator was briefly the site of a major traffic jam.

"Bye!" all of the women called out to each other as the elevator doors closed.

"How strange!" said Opal when the three women were alone in the elevator.

"That they all seemed really happy that Bob is going to be okay?" asked Marjorie.

"Rose and Hazel are very solicitous of Evelyn," said Opal.

"She's been ill, Opal," noted Essie, "and undergoing chemotherapy. Did you see how she was walking? Rose and Hazel had to practically hold her up and they were the ones with the canes—not her."

"I guess that's it," agreed Opal. When they reached the family room, they saw Fay tapping away at the computer keyboard.

"My goodness, look at her go," said Marjorie. "What is she doing?"

"Maybe she's found some more dirt on Violet," offered Essie. The three rolled their carts over to where Fay was working diligently at the terminal. Fay turned and saw her friends had arrived. She hit the "print" button and the wheels of the printer behind the monitor started to spin and soon dozens of pages of printed material began pouring forth.

"What is all this?" asked Essie, gathering the pages together.

"Why don't you take it and read it, Essie?" suggested Opal. "I should probably see that Fay gets back to her room now." Opal tapped Fay on the shoulder and motioned that they should leave. Fay rolled the wheels on her chair back and then forward until she was aimed in the direction of the elevator and the two friends headed into the open chamber with the door closing behind them.

"Do you want me to read some of that, Essie?" asked Marjorie, pointing to the sheets of paper in Essie's hands.

"No," said Essie, shaking her head. "I asked for it, so I'd better read it. I can't imagine that Fay actually found any real dirt on Violet, but it'll give me something to do tonight before bed."

"I'll see you tomorrow," said Marjorie and she headed off down her hallway.

Essie straightened up her pile of papers, tucked them inside her walker's compartment and rolled herself down her hallway to her apartment. Once inside, she sat down in her armchair and began to glance at the papers Fay had printed.

She wasn't exactly certain what all of the verbiage was. The tops of most of the pages were labeled "Minutes" and there was a date on each page. One page had a heading "Board of Directors' Annual Meeting, Happy Haven Assisted Living Facility." The date on each page was "June 15th, 1995." *Hmm*, thought Essie. Quite possibly, the minutes from this Board meeting might indicate just what the flack was over the hiring of Violet Hendrickson— why one Board member wanted to hire her—and one didn't. *Did one of the Board members know about Violet's DUI? Or her past as a college protestor?* Unfortunately, the minutes were written in boring prose—and proved very difficult to read with lots of "therefores" and "whereas's." Essie had completed about three out of the dozens of pages Fay had printed, when her nighttime aide, Connie, arrived to get her ready for bed and give her her bedtime meds.

# Chapter Twenty-One

*"We've put more effort into helping folks reach old age than into helping them enjoy it."*
—Frank A. Clark

When Essie awoke the next morning, she was chastising herself for not finishing reading the printed minutes from the Board of Directors' meeting. She'd left the pile of papers on her end table in the living room. Now, she probably wouldn't have any time because Prudence was coming over right after breakfast to take her to her doctor appointment. DeeDee's voice called out and soon her lively Italian morning assistant was cajoling her out from under her warm duvet and whipping Essie into her daily uniform in her typically efficient yet bubbly manner.

"DeeDee," said Essie, as she held up her foot to get her shoe laces tied, "what is your opinion of Violet Hendrickson?"

"Old sourpuss? Ooops, I mean, our Director," chuckled DeeDee, a hand over her mouth.

"You're not too fond of her?" asked Essie.

"She doesn't have a very touchy-feely manner," noted DeeDee, smacking her lips in an exaggerated fashion and then quickly placing her finger to her lips in the "shh" gesture.

"Does all the staff feel the same?" continued Essie.

"Most of us, I guess," answered DeeDee, now helping Essie up and to her walker.

"What about Sue Barber, the Social Director?" queried Essie as she shuffled out to her living room.

"Oh, her!" scoffed DeeDee, bringing Essie her pills. "She's just her flunky."

"Flunky?" said Essie, astonished.

"Yeah," replied DeeDee. "That woman adores Violet. Why, I'll never know. Violet is such a cold fish. Why she ever wanted to work at an assisted living facility—let alone got to be a director of one—is beyond me."

"Her job has never been in jeopardy?"

"I guess she must know people in high places, if you know what I mean," said DeeDee rolling her eyes.

"Does the job pay well?"

"Essie, let's just say that for what she does, it pays really well," answered DeeDee.

"You mean she's incompetent."

"More like superfluous," responded DeeDee. "This place is a well-oiled machine. You know it. We have a great staff and we're well paid compared to lots of facilities. Violet is really just a figurehead who sits in her office and greets visiting dignitaries."

"I saw her handle a rather sticky situation yesterday rather well," suggested Essie tentatively.

"Oh, she can be diplomatic. Don't get me wrong. She knows how to sweet talk and persuade. Unfortunately, she tends to use those skills more for her own benefit than for Happy Haven."

"Hmm," said Essie.

"You're all set, Missie," said DeeDee, giving Essie a hug. "Now, you're not going to repeat all of this to Violet, are you?"

"Absolutely not, DeeDee," agreed Essie. "And thanks for your honesty." She smiled and waved goodbye to her aide as DeeDee headed out the door. Essie sat in her chair, her clipboard of crossword puzzles in her lap, and contemplated her next move. Violet Hendrickson required more investigation; that was for sure. As she had some time before breakfast, Essie reached over to the stack of printed sheets next to her telephone where she had left them the previous evening. For some reason, Fay seemed to think that these minutes held some important information. Or maybe, Fay was just dreaming. Maybe she just found Violet's name listed somewhere and printed everything she could find whether it was meaningful or not. She looked at the page on the top of the pile.

Flipping on her table lamp, she brought the small print as close to her eyes as possible and started to read.

The minutes indicated a rather heated discussion about the finances at Happy Haven.   She really didn't understand what the Board members were arguing about, but it seemed to concern investments in the facility's holdings.   Some Board members believed that Happy Haven needed to diversify their holdings more and other members disagreed.   Page after page indicated motions and counter-motions regarding changes to the portfolio.   It was excruciatingly boring—sort of like listening to Darrell, her financial advisor, ramble on about the stock market for hours at a time.   After about six or seven pages of this, she came to a spot where one Board member made a motion to consider filling the Director's position at Happy Haven.   He noted that the present director was retiring in several months and that they would be obligated to replace him.   The minutes indicated that several candidates had applied and had been interviewed.   The top three candidates for the position were listed in the minutes.   One of those candidates was Violet Hendrickson.   After this, the minutes indicated an intense discussion about the three candidates.   *Ah*, thought Essie, *now it's getting juicy*.

"Mr. James Abernathy moved that the Board select Margaret Peterson as the new Director of Happy Haven," indicated the minutes. Then discussion from fellow members was recorded in the minutes.   Ms. Peterson's qualifications were discussed critically.  Following this scrutiny of the first candidate, the same routine was utilized for a second candidate—a Priscilla Hardy. *Finally*, said Essie to herself, *the Board came to their final candidate—Violet Hendrickson.*

"Ms. Hendrickson," read the minutes, "has the educational qualifications and the experience for this position."   Essie read then about Violet's background, her major in college, her work experience, and a list of her former jobs.  She was duly impressed. Even so, Violet's qualifications didn't seem any more stellar than those of the other two candidates.

At one point, one Board member asked, "Should we not re-interview these three women, seeing as how they all appear to be equally qualified?"

Another Board member responded, "Since they're all equally qualified, does it really matter which one we choose?"

Essie stopped and reread this remark to be sure she had read it correctly the first time. Yes, it appeared the Board didn't seem to be all that concerned about their choice of director for Happy Haven.

"I move," said one Board member, as indicated in the minutes, "that we offer the position of Executive Director to Violet Hendrickson." *Why*? Essie asked as she continued to read.

"I have no problem with the Hendrickson woman," said another. "Either of the three would be fine. Their qualifications are all relatively comparable. I don't think we really need to interview them again."

*So, why Violet*? Essie wondered. She continued to read.

The Board member who had moved to hire Violet added in the minutes, "I knew Ms. Hendrickson's father years ago. A good family—and a well-placed one. She has a nice social standing—the other two, I don't know much about their families." Several other members offered confirmation for this analysis in the minutes, making their remarks sound as if Violet's social position and family background were of greater importance in qualifying her for the Director's position than her own education and experience.

*Hmm*, thought Essie. *I guess they either ignored that DUI or didn't know about it.* Even so, she realized, all of this had happened years ago and Violet had been their Director for the entire time that Essie had been a resident, so for all she knew, Violet was a sterling Director compared to other assisted living facility directors around the country. Could she—should she—hold one indiscretion against the woman? A DUI was not exactly elder abuse. But she couldn't help but wonder at the cavalier attitude of this Board of Directors—as evidenced by these minutes—the very people who should be most concerned about the welfare of the residents—just doling out the top job to someone based on their family's social standing. Or at least to Essie's understanding, that's what appeared to have happened.

The intercom interjected into her musings. "Residents, good morning. It's seven-thirty and time for the first seating at breakfast. We have fresh cinnamon rolls today!"

Essie smirked. They have fresh cinnamon rolls every day, she thought. She roused herself from her chair, made a fast detour to her bathroom because all the water she had swallowed to take her pills had seeped right through her, and then out she rolled to the dining hall.

## Chapter Twenty-two

*"After the age of 80, everything reminds you of something else."*
—Lowell Thomas

After breakfast, she hurried back to her apartment to brush her teeth and visit her toilet a second time. Just as she was walking out of her bathroom, her daughter Prudence arrived.

"Mom!" called Prudence. "I'm here! Are you ready?"

"Pru!" greeted Essie, "What's the weather like? Do I need a jacket?"

"Just your light coat, I think," answered Prudence. She opened Essie's small living room closet and removed her blue raincoat and slipped it on her mother. "I've already signed you out, so we can just go."

"A long trip today, right?" asked Essie.

"I know," agreed Prudence. "But, Mom, the trees are in bloom and there are so many of them between here and Elmwood. You'll love it!" She guided Essie out of her apartment and out through the main entrance. At the front of the building, Prudence helped Essie into the front passenger seat of her little white Toyota, and then quickly dismantled Essie's walker and stuffed it in her trunk. Then she slid into the driver's seat and the two women took off amidst a lively conversation about weather and catching up on family events.

"Oh my!" shouted Essie as they hit the highway on the way to Elmwood, "How beautiful!" And truly, the road seemed to be lined with parade watchers and those watchers were all festooned with garlands of flowers. Essie was entranced. She so seldom had the opportunity to get outside of Happy Haven, that when she did, she always enjoyed the natural scenery.

"A perfect April day!" exclaimed Prudence. Soon, they had arrived at the doctor's office. Actually, it was a small brick building located conveniently along the highway. Prudence parked directly across from the entrance and shortly the two women were inside and waiting in the doctor's lobby.

Almost immediately, the nurse called Essie's name and she wheeled herself down the narrow hallway and around several corners into the small office. Prudence followed and the two women seated themselves before the doctor's impressive desk. They always enjoyed commenting on the doctor's array of unusual artwork on the walls and strange sculptures on her desk. However, today, they didn't have time for that because the doctor entered from another door and immediately seated herself at the desk.

"Miss Essie," said the plain female physician with her hair pulled back into a loose bun, "how have you been?"

"Fine, Dr. Payne," said Essie politely, "Just fine."

"Now, let's see, you're at Happy Haven, right?" Essie always thought it was unusual that she was seeing this doctor for, among other things, memory loss and the doctor never seemed to remember anything about her.

"Right," responded Essie.

"And how are you feeling?" continued the doctor, looking from her folder on her desk up at Essie.

"Fine, doctor."

"Eating well?"

"Oh, yes."

"Getting exercise?"

"Oh, yes."

"What about activities?" the doctor continued.

"I play Bingo," offered Essie.

"Really?" queried the doctor, the tip of her pen between her teeth. "Do you ever win?"

"Once in a while."

"That must be exciting!"

"It is!" said Essie. "One of our residents won the other night and he collapsed and fell into a coma!"

"When he won at Bingo?" she asked.

"Yes. Well, not right when he won," Essie said, correcting herself.

"Oh?" asked the doctor.

"No, now that I think about it," said Essie, thinking hard, "he was fine when he won. It wasn't until he went up to claim his prize that he collapsed."

"What was the prize?" chuckled the doctor. "A Ferrari?"

"No, just a dollar bill," said Essie.

"I can't imagine him getting all that excited over a dollar bill," noted the doctor, "unless, of course, he was really poverty stricken."

"He's definitely not poor," said Essie.

"Then it must have been something else," suggested the doctor.

"Yes," agreed Essie.

The doctor moved on. "How's your memory, Essie?"

"Fine."

"What's your name?"

"Essie Cobb."

"How old are you?"

"Ninety."

"She just had her birthday," interjected Prudence. "It was a great party!"

"I'm sure it was!" said the doctor, smiling. "Essie, do you know the date?"

"Uh, Tuesday, April 5, 2011."

"That's right. What about the President?"

"What about him?" retorted Essie.

"I mean, who is the President?" asked the doctor. Essie responded correctly. "What about the governor?"

"Who?" asked Essie, looking flustered.

"Doctor," said Prudence quickly, "I don't think it's that she doesn't remember the name of the governor. It's more that she's just not interested in politics."

"I see," said the doctor. "There must be a lot going on over at Happy Haven that keeps you occupied."

"Oh, yes," said Essie.

"That's good," said the doctor. Essie smiled. "Essie, do you have any questions?"

"Do you know anything about Medilogicos?" Essie asked abruptly.

The doctor laughed. "My goodness, Essie. That's quite a question. Medilogicos is a large medical software company."

"Are they—uh—successful?" asked Essie.

"I'd say they are," the doctor said, smiling. "We use their services. Truthfully, they've revolutionized a lot of medical testing and how we interact with patients."

"Good," said Essie. "Then their executives are probably not poor."

"I would think not," said the doctor. "Have you heard of Bill Gates?"

"They're as rich as him?"

"Not quite, but believe me—Medilogicos is well known in the medical community."

"That's good to hear, doctor," noted Essie.

"I guess we'll just keep things the way they are then, Essie; okay? I'll call in renewals for all your meds."

"Good," replied Essie.

"And I'll see you in six months."

"Okay," agreed Essie. The doctor beamed at Essie, shook her hand, and then exited out the back door in the office. Prudence and Essie rose and ambled out into the lobby. Essie waited as Prudence made her six month appointment. She was thinking about what she had talked about with the doctor—not about her health or memory. None of that. She was thinking about the conversation about Bob's collapse at Bingo and how he hadn't fallen right when he got the Bingo; he had fallen when he went up and claimed his dollar bill. That didn't make a lot of sense now that she thought about it. If Bob was all that upset—about Ben Jericho or Violet Hendrickson—or whoever or whatever was worrying him—you'd think that the added stress of actually winning would send him over the top—anxiety-wise. You wouldn't think that he'd be just fine during that exciting part and manage to walk all the way over to the center of the room and reach out and grab that dollar bill—and only then hit the floor.

Prudence came into the lobby.

"Let's go, Mom!" she said and the women headed out of the doctor's office and back to Happy Haven—the scene of enough excitement to keep Essie's memory and mental faculties in top form for a long time. Gerontologists! Ha!

## Chapter Twenty-three

*"Those who love deeply never grow old; they may die of old age, but they die young."*
—Sir Arthur Pinero

When she returned from the doctor's office, it was still relatively early in the morning. Essie checked back in, said goodbye to her daughter, and dropped off her coat. Then after a quickie (meaning a quick potty break), she headed out into the family room. None of her three compatriots were in sight, so she continued rolling towards the back of the room and down the narrow hallway leading towards the chapel.

As she slid inside the small room and her eyes eventually adjusted to the darkness, she observed a figure in one of the front pews. From the colorful scarf on her head, she knew it was Evelyn Cudahy. Evelyn's head was bowed and Essie did not wish to disturb her. She pulled her walker over to the side of a back pew and sat down and waited. After a few moments, Evelyn looked up and rose. Turning and starting to walk down the chapel's center aisle, she saw Essie sitting quietly in the back.

"Essie," said Evelyn, walking slowly over and sitting in the pew in front of Essie. "We meet again."

"Hello, Evelyn," said Essie. "Are you feeling better than last night?"

"Yes, as a matter of fact, I'm doing remarkably well today," she said joyously. "I believe that last night I was just overcome with exhaustion and concern."

"For Bob?"

"Yes," she answered, "of course, for Bob."

"And today you're greatly improved."

"Yes," she replied, then added quietly, "I spoke with him just a little while ago on the phone. Oh, Essie, he's well enough to call me."

"How wonderful!"

"You just don't know!" said Evelyn. "I didn't know that I'd ever talk to him again." Tears welled in her eyes and she pulled a rolled up tissue from her pocket and wiped them.

"You are certainly a very good friend to Bob, Evelyn."

"Essie," said Evelyn. "Essie, I'm looking at you and I believe you are very smart, very intuitive." Essie remained quiet, listening. "I think you know, don't you?"

"About you and Bob? I think you and Bob are more than just friends, Evelyn," responded Essie.

Evelyn's tears welled again and her nose began to run. Her tissue was soon working overtime.

"We are," she replied. "Essie, it's only a secret because we were waiting for the right moment. And then Bob collapsed at Bingo and—oh—it's just been a nightmare. What was supposed to be wonderful turned into this nightmare."

"A secret?" asked Essie.

"Bob and I are married," she whispered.

"Married?" responded Essie, shocked. *So Bev was right*.

"Just a few days before the Bingo episode, we went to city hall and eloped."

"Oh, my!" said Essie. "I had no idea."

"No," said Evelyn. "Not many people do—just Hazel and Rose. They helped us with the wedding. They've been wonderful. Hazel's with me almost all the time to assist me with my chemo. Rose has been visiting Bob in the hospital because I'm not allowed to."

"But if you're his wife, surely they'd let you in," argued Essie.

"It's not that," explained Evelyn. "I'm not allowed in for my sake, because of the chemo. They won't let me in that part of the hospital."

"But you got to speak to him today—that's wonderful!"

"Yes," agreed Evelyn. "I feel so confident now that he'll recuperate and be back here soon."

"Did he say anything about what upset him so before Bingo? You know, you said he had something important he wanted to tell you."

"He didn't tell me on the phone, but he did say to be careful."

"Do you think whatever he's worried about is what was worrying him the afternoon before Bingo? You know, the thing he wanted to tell you about but didn't get a chance."

"I don't know why he said to be careful, Essie. I don't know what he wanted to tell me after Bingo."

"Do you think maybe he discovered something?"

"Like what?"

"I don't know," replied Essie, not wanting to reveal her hand, "maybe something about a staff member or maybe somebody from outside had contacted him. You never know."

"I guess he's just worried about me and my chemo, but my oncologist says that I'm doing well."

"That's wonderful, Evelyn," said Essie, touching her arm which rested now on the top of the pew in front of Essie. "Did Bob say any more about what the doctors think caused him to collapse?"

"He did say something strange. He said they found some unusual substance in his bloodstream. They don't know what it is. He said they didn't know if it was the cause of his coma, but evidently they're still investigating. Whatever it is—or was—it appears to have drained from his system. It's actually probably lucky that he collapsed and was hospitalized when he was because they were able to give him a transfusion and that was no doubt helpful in getting rid of this substance."

"No doubt," agreed Essie, contemplating the information Evelyn had just imparted to her.

"When he returns, then you'll announce that you're married?"

"We plan to, yes."

"We'll have to throw a big party for you!"

"That would be lovely, but please keep it very low key," she begged. "We both just need some peace and quiet."

"Then, that's what you will get!" she said, patting Evelyn's hand. With that, Essie bid farewell to the new bride and headed out of the chapel and back to her room. She had a lot to contemplate before lunch.

# Chapter Twenty-four

*"Middle age is when your age starts to show around your middle."*
—Bob Hope

Lunch was uneventful. Essie, Opal, Marjorie, and Fay dined on chef salads and homemade rolls. They waved at Evelyn, Rose, and Hazel when the three women from Bob Weiderley's table arrived shortly after they did. Essie was itching to tell her tablemates about Bob and Evelyn's secret wedding but true to her word, she kept quiet.

"Where were you all morning?" asked Marjorie. "I looked for you at trivia."

"Pru took me to my gerontologist," Essie responded, not adding that she also spent time extracting information from Evelyn Cudahy. "I'm healthy as a horse."

"I've known some pretty sickly horses in my day," claimed Opal who had grown up on a farm.

"My old person doc says I'm a healthy old person! There! Is that better?"

"What about your memory?" queried Opal. "You always forget what you ate the very next day."

"So?" scowled Essie. "Who cares if I remember what I eat? It's not important."

"Oh, it could be important, Essie," explained Marjorie in her sweet elementary school teacher guise. "Just imagine if you weren't supposed to eat something you were allergic to and you forgot if you ate it or not!"

"What!" Essie sputtered. "You two are ridiculous. Fay, you have the right idea. Just sleep through lunch!"

Fay opened an eye when she heard her name. When she saw that her friends were embroiled in a row, she quickly went back to sleep.

"I found out something!" announced Opal, when the hubbub had quieted. "Violet recently got a raise. A big one."

"How'd you find that out?" asked Essie.

"My morning aide, Jerold, heard it from another aide who heard it from another aide."

"That's hearsay," said Marjorie. "It might not be true."

"It probably is," said Essie. "And for what does she get a raise? It's not as if she does anything."

"Essie! Why are you all of a sudden so opposed to Violet?"

"Because," noted Essie, "I finished reading all those minutes from that Board of Directors' meeting back before she was hired. The minutes that Fay printed for us from the computer. Turns out . . .—" She leaned in and Marjorie and Opal leaned in to hear.

"Turns out she was selected from three candidates."

"So?" asked Marjorie. "She must have been the best of the three."

"The best of the three as far as having a good family name and highly placed social standing," said Essie.

"What?" shrieked Opal.

"You heard me. I read those minutes and it was quite obvious that those Board members had only gone through the motions of interviewing those candidates. Violet evidently came from the more prominent family and that appeared to be the deciding factor."

"Not her credentials?" asked Opal.

"Oh, her credentials were as good as the other two candidates, at least that's what the minutes claim, but wouldn't you think if you had three equally qualified candidates, you'd want to interview them more so that you could select the best one—versus just picking the one with the best social standing?" Essie was adamant in her disgust.

"They must have made a reasonably good decision," noted Marjorie. "Violet's been here over twelve years without any problems."

"Until now," said Essie.

"You mean . . .—" suggested Opal.

"This episode with Bob is not over. Mark my words," argued Essie.

"But Essie," pleaded Marjorie, "he's out of the coma. He'll probably be released. How is Violet responsible? She called the ambulance. It seems to me she played everything by the book."

"Hmmm," pondered Essie. "We'll see."

"What else could there be?" asked Opal.

"Poison," whispered Essie.

"What?" whispered Marjorie. "I thought we discussed this before and you gave up on that ridiculous idea!"

"It's not ridiculous," answered Essie. "I just spoke to Evelyn this morning. She talked to Bob on the phone a bit ago and he told her that the doctors found a suspicious substance in his bloodstream. They don't know what it is—or was—because it's apparently drained from his system now."

"Do they think this substance is what caused him to collapse?" asked Opal.

"They don't know," said Essie, "but they're investigating. Now what does that suggest to you?"

"I don't know," answered Marjorie, "but it seems to me they're going to need a lot more information before they can pin it on Violet—if that's where you're going. I mean as far as I can tell, Violet hasn't had any personal contact with Bob recently until after he had collapsed."

"I know," said Essie. "I haven't figured out all the angles yet, but I'm working on them."

"Good luck with that, Detective Cobb," said Opal, shaking her head.

And indeed, Detective Essie Cobb was working on the angles.

"Fay," she called out to the little woman snoring quietly in her wheelchair. Fay nodded her head and squinted her eyes open.

"Fay, can you get on that computer this afternoon and look up information on poisons?  Particularly poisons that might cause a coma.  Find out how it might be administered.  Find out about where someone could get it—how dangerous it is.  You know, Fay.  I know you know, Fay.  I know you know what we need.  So go get it, girl!"

Fay smiled at Essie, yawned, and then fell back to sleep.

"She doesn't understand," noted Marjorie.

"Yes, she does," said Essie.  "She just has her own way of responding."

The women had finished their salads and all were feeling rather cheerful as the dining hall was beaming with light from a lovely April day, and an entire band of songbirds were chirping outside the dining hall window.  They all elected to indulge in the proffered apricot mousse cake.  Santos delivered the scrumptious desserts with a wink to the members of what Essie knew was his favorite table. The women made short work of the four little slices of condensed calories.

## Chapter Twenty-five

*"To get back my youth I would do anything in the world, except take exercise,*
*get up early, or be respectable."*
—Oscar Wilde

The four friends were passing through the main lobby after their pleasant, leisurely lunch.  Opal, Marjorie, and Essie were just saying good-bye to Fay who wheeled herself off to the computer in the family room.  *How nice it is*, thought Essie, *to have a researcher.  Fay certainly knows how to mine that Internet busines*s.

At that moment, Sue Barber, wearing a light jacket and carrying a purse over her shoulder, came barreling through the lobby from the main entrance.

"Oh, there you are!" she called out to Essie and her friends. "We were almost ready to leave without you."

"What?" said Essie.  Opal and Marjorie looked at each other curiously.

"Don't you ladies remember?" Sue asked, shaking her finger at the three women.  She zipped over to the front counter and grabbed a clipboard.  "Remember, you girls signed up for the field trip to the Reardon botanical gardens today!"  She waved the sign-up sheet with their signatures under their noses.

"Oh, Sue," said Marjorie sheepishly.  "I'm not really dressed for a field trip."

"Me either," claimed Opal.

"Nonsense," responded Sue.  "You both are dressed just fine. The weather is perfect.  Come along now.  You've made us delay long enough.  Let's go.  The driver is waiting."

"You mean right now? This instant?" cried Essie. "The bus is here?"

"Right out there," she said, motioning to the front door. "Can't you see it?" She waved her arms at the big yellow school bus sitting under the overhang on the front drive.

"I'm not at all ready," continued Essie. "I'd have to go clean up and use the bathroom."

"Don't be silly," said Sue firmly. "You can do that when you get to the gardens. They're just a short drive away. Now hurry! The whole group has been sitting on the bus waiting for the three of you!"

Essie looked at Opal and then at Marjorie as if to say "*do you have any other excuses?*"

"But, I . . . — I . . . —" stammered Essie.

"Let's go!" Sue ordered. With that, she herded the women and their walkers out the main entrance as if they were a head of cattle. The bus driver quickly hopped down from his seat and helped Sue load the walkers into the luggage bins on the side of the bus. Then the driver and Sue urged the women up the two steps and into the bus. This was a much greater task than loading the walkers. Essie moaned with each step, threatening to faint from exertion. Opal and Marjorie complained almost as much. When all three women were finally on the bus and seated at the very back (the only seats left), all the residents gave a loud round of applause. Then the driver started up the spunky little vehicle, released the emergency brake with a start that sent Marjorie flying down the center aisle, and with a jerk, the field trip to the botanical gardens was on its way.

"Thanks a lot, Essie," grumbled Opal to her pal on her left. "How did you ever get us into this? A bus trip is the last thing I wanted to do today."

"You?" sneered Essie. "I have to pee so badly I'll probably send a stream of urine all the way to the front of this stupid bus in the next second."

"At least the two of you are able to stay seated!" cursed Marjorie. "Every time the damn thing stops, I fall on the floor!"

"Where did that annoying Sue Barber go anyway?" asked Essie. "I don't see her."

"She's sitting up near the driver," said Marjorie.

"She's probably got a crush on him," observed Opal. "That's probably why she schedules so many field trips."

"Are we there yet? I really have to pee," squeaked Essie, crossing her thin legs and sqeezing her eyes shut.

"Complain! Complain! Is that all you two can do?" said Marjorie. "The other residents seem to be enjoying themselves."

"They have better bladder control," countered Essie, grimacing.

"Hang on, Essie," said Opal encouragingly. "Oh, look! We're pulling into the gardens!"

And sure enough, the driver made a sharp left turn (causing Marjorie to slide precipitously into Opal) into the Reardon Botanical Gardens. The entrance was a spectacle of begonias, petunias, and roses winding upward around the twenty-foot spikes of a tall, wrought iron fence. As the bus came to a sudden and bladder-squeezing stop, Sue Barber stood where she had been seated at the front of the bus.

"Now, residents," she announced, "enjoy your visit to the Reardon Botanical Gardens. It's now 1:30 p.m. Please be back on the bus by 3 o'clock which is when we will depart for Happy Haven." She bounded off the bus and assisted the driver in unlocking the luggage compartment. They removed walkers and then began helping the residents down the short flight of steps.

"We would be at the very back," said Essie as the three women waited at the end of the line to exit the bus. She looked out the bus window and saw that Sue and the driver were totally occupied with helping each resident depart.

"Is that where Sue was sitting?" Essie asked Opal, as she pointed to the front seat opposite the driver.

"I believe so," answered Opal. "Why do you care?"

"I'm just curious about something," replied Essie, scooting onto the seat she had just mentioned. Sue Barber had left her purse on her seat—obviously so it wouldn't get in her way while she helped the residents debus. Essie picked up Sue's carryall satchel and unobtrusively lifted the top flap. Peeking in the interior, she stuck in her hand and shuffled the items around, trying to see what lay inside.

"Essie!" cried Marjorie, "What are you doing?"

"That's not your purse!" said Opal.

"Quiet!" whispered Essie. "I'm just checking to see if she has any tissue."

"I have tissue, Essie," said Marjorie. "In my walker. You can have some when we get down."

"Never mind," said Essie. "My goodness, look at this." She carefully brought out a small plastic bag containing what appeared to be a folded up dollar bill.

"What's that?" asked Marjorie.

"What does it look like?" retorted Essie.

"Like something that doesn't belong to you, Essie," snorted Opal, as she grabbed the little bag and shoved it back into the purse. "For heaven's sake, what are you doing?"

"Just investigating," said Essie. "Oh, look, everybody is all almost out of the bus. Let's go."

As Essie hit the ground, she said, "Where's the restroom?"

The driver, who'd obviously brought seniors to the botanical gardens before, pointed out a big, square, grey building at the top of a small incline a few yards off to the left—just inside the entrance to the gardens.

"Great!" she replied. "Don't anyone get in my way!" With that, she pushed her walker at breakneck speed as fast as her little feet and her well-tied sneakers would carry her. Opal and Marjorie smiled politely at the driver and especially politely at Sue Barber whose purse Essie had just burgled. Then they too started for the public restroom building.

"She's a character," said the bus driver to Sue Barber.

"That's putting it mildly," agreed Sue.

## Chapter Twenty-six

*"So much has been said and sung of beautiful young girls; why don't somebody wake up to the beauty of old women?*
—Harriet Beecher Stowe

Essie shoved open the rickety old metal door of the women's side of the public restroom building with the front of her walker. The door rubbed and scraped over the linoleum floor and finally slammed against the tile wall. The noise reverberated with a loud echo but Essie ignored it and everything else as she hurriedly rushed her walker down the line of five enclosed toilets to the compartment at the far end, labeled "handicapped." She quickly drove her walker through the door of the special toilet stall. Then, grabbing an old wadded up tissue from her pocket, she gingerly shoved the rusted lock on the toilet door—or attempted to shove the rusted lock into its holder.

"Stupid lock!" she yelled at the fixture as the door to the restroom opened.

"Essie!" called out a voice she recognized as Marjorie's.

"Guard this door, Marjorie!" shouted Essie. "I can't get the lock to work!"

"Okay, but hurry up!" said Marjorie. "I have to go too!"

"Me too!" added Opal, right behind her.

"Lord's gourds!" mumbled Essie, ignoring the door and positioning her walker in front of the toilet. As she looked down at the toilet, she gasped. A film of muck covered the seat and rust encrusted the handle. "Wonderful," she commented.

"What?" called out Marjorie. "Are you hurrying? Opal and I both have to go and we can't get our walkers into any of these other stalls."

"Just stay where you are and guard my door!"

Essie looked for the toilet paper dispenser so she could clean the toilet, but unfortunately there was no roll of paper in the dispenser and no spare roll to be found anywhere in the stall.

"Marjorie, go into another stall and get me some toilet paper," demanded Essie.

"Are you done already?" asked Marjorie scooting into the neighboring stall. "I can't get in this stall, Essie. Wait, I'll walk in but I'll have to hold onto the walls."

"Here, Marjorie," suggested Opal, "let me do it. I'm taller." She grabbed the handles of Marjorie's walker and leaned sideways into the stall where a roll of paper was balanced somewhat precariously on top of the dispenser.

"Did you get it?" called Essie. She hobbled from one foot to another trying to contain the urge to urinate.

"Just a minute!" responded Opal. "Yes, I've got it! Now, what should I do with it?"

"Just roll it under the door."

"Really? Okay, Essie, if you say so!" said Opal, as she bent low and gave the cylinder of paper a gentle shove under the handicapped stall.

"Opal, are you a bowler?" asked Marjorie in admiration. "That was smooth!"

"I was on a company league once," replied a smiling Opal.

Meanwhile, Essie, inside the roomy handicapped stall, had grabbed the roll of paper and peeled it open and was using large handfuls to wipe the seat dry.

"This paper is hard as sandpaper," she complained. "I don't like the thought of rubbing it on my tush."

"Quit complaining, Essie," yelled Opal, "and hurry up!"

When the toilet seat was appropriately dry, Essie pulled down her trousers and lowered herself in place.

"This seat is too low!" she yelled.

"It's higher than the floor, Goldilocks!" responded Marjorie, "Just hurry up!"

The two women outside the stall heard a sudden flow of liquid and a relieved "ah" emanate from inside.

"Ouch!" called Essie.

"What's wrong?" yelled Opal.

"This paper is ripping my skin!"

"Hurry up, Essie!" said Marjorie, doing a little dance in front of her walker.

At long last, the sound of flushing noted the end of their vigil. Essie pulled back the stall door and rolled her walker out. Marjorie immediately started to push her walker into the stall.

"I need to go more!" said Opal.

"I got here first!" argued Marjorie, zipping in front of Opal and slamming the door in her face. Essie rolled over to the row of sinks across from the toilets.

"Wonderful!" she cried. "No toilet paper! Now no paper towels!"

"Do they have a hand blower?" asked Marjorie, now efficiently at work inside the stall.

"I don't see one," said Essie. "How am I going to wash my hands?"

"Hurry up, Marjorie!" called Opal with urgency, still standing guard in front of the handicapped stall.

Essie poked at a soap dispenser only partially filled with a liquid the color of flamingos.

"Eeek," she grimaced. "Look at this creepy looking soap." She tentatively pushed the dispenser knob and a glob of the material squirted into her palm. "Yuck, it's disgusting."

"It's soap!" said Opal, behind her. "How disgusting can it be?"

"I'm done!" announced Marjorie, opening the stall door with a satisfied look. Opal rushed past her friend and into the stall.

"You stay there, Marjorie," ordered Opal. "Don't go anywhere."

"Opal," said Marjorie, "there's no one else in here. So what if the door's unlocked? Essie and I aren't going to break in while you're using the bathroom."

"I just want the same protection that the two of you had," said Opal with a whine.

Marjorie wheeled over to the sinks and reached out to wash her hands.  Essie was still rubbing her hands together with the pink goop.

"Look at this stuff, Marjorie," she said as she nudged her sprightly friend.

Marjorie glanced at the soap on Essie's hands and turned on the faucet.

Yikes!" she screamed.  "It's all cold water!"

"You have to let it warm up before you just go and stick your hands under the flow," suggested Essie.

"I don't have to do that in my bathroom," said Marjorie.

"This isn't your bathroom, Marjorie!" said Essie.  The sound of another flush announced the completion of Opal's bathroom visit and soon the tallest member of the group had joined the two shorter women at the sinks.  As all three ladies stood in line behind their walkers staring into the mirrors and washing their hands, Essie couldn't help thinking how much the three of them looked like some bizarre elderly vocal group—maybe "The Walkers"!

"Finally," said Marjorie, looking at her friends in the mirrors.

"We are rather cute, aren't we?" noted Essie as she smiled into the mirror.

"Speak for yourself," scowled Opal.  "Cute is not an appropriate adjective for women our age."

"I can't help it," continued Essie, "when my bladder is empty I feel like I can conquer the world!"

"Essie," said Marjorie, shaking her finger at her friend's image in the mirror, "let's don't conquer the world—let's just figure out what happened to Bob.  Remember!  That's our project."

"Project!" scoffed Opal. "You make it sound like we're a bunch of Girl Scouts, Marjorie."

The women continued to stand before the mirrors, leaning on their walkers, and talking--even though they all had finished washing their hands quite thoroughly.

"Essie," said Marjorie, "just what was all that in the bus?  When you opened Sue Barber's purse?"

"I was looking for clues," Essie said cryptically.

"And you found some sort of plastic bag with some money in it," added Opal. "What kind of clue is that? It shows that Sue is very protective of her money?"

"Or she's very frugal and likes to keep her money stashed away for special purchases," suggested Marjorie.

"Or," noted Essie, "she's saving the dollar bill that she offered to Bob Weiderley as a Bingo prize the night he collapsed."

"Why would she do that?" asked Marjorie.

"Indeed," answered Essie. "Why?"

"There could be all sorts of reasons, Essie," suggested Opal. "I mean, maybe she sets aside a certain number of dollar bills to use on Bingo night and keeps them in a plastic bag in her purse. You know, so she doesn't mix up her own money with the Bingo money."

"That's probably it," agreed Marjorie.

"Or," suggested Essie, "she needs to prevent anyone from getting a hold of that dollar bill that she gave to Bob right before he collapsed."

"Why?" asked Marjorie.

"Because she poisoned it!" said Essie.

"What?" cried Opal. "You've got to be kidding!"

"Sue Barber didn't poison Bob!" added Marjorie.

"How do we know she didn't?" asked Essie, leaning back from the mirrors and speaking now to her friends face-to-face.

"Why?" asked Opal.

"Yes, Essie," agreed Marjorie, "Why would Sue do such a thing? She has no reason to hurt Bob."

"Not that we know," answered Essie. She pushed her walker away from the sink and started to turn it toward the restroom door.

"You're letting your imagination run away with you, Essie," said Opal, now following her friend onto the grounds of the botanical gardens.

"I agree," said Marjorie, following the other two women as they gathered their front wheels together immediately in front of the public restroom, the bright blue signs indicating 'male' and 'female' standing guard over their discussion.

"Marjorie, Opal," said Essie, looking directly at her friends, "there's no reason for Sue Barber to save that dollar bill—to keep it protected in a sealed plastic bag in her purse—if it were merely part of funds that were used for Bingo prizes. Something else is going on. She saved that one dollar for a reason."

"If it were poisoned, surely she'd get rid of it," offered Marjorie.

"Not necessarily," added Essie. "Maybe she intends to use it again. I mean, Bob is still alive."

"How gruesome, Essie," said Opal. "And if that dollar bill was poisoned, how did she hand it to Bob without getting poisoned herself?

"And how do you poison someone with a dollar bill? Just by touching it?" asked Marjorie. "That must be a really potent poison."

"Which would explain why she's keeping it in a plastic bag," answered Essie.

"I just don't see what motive Sue would have to hurt Bob," mused Opal, grinding her teeth over her bottom lip. "He's such a nice man."

"Such a nice *rich* man," added Essie. "Maybe she had some scheme to get his millions."

"His five millions," added Marjorie, caught up in the excitement of their discussion.

"So," said Opal calmly, "we now have three suspects."

"Three?" asked Marjorie.

"Sue, Violet, and this Ben Jericho," listed Opal.

"Yes," agreed Essie, smiling. "I'm not certain that all three have a motive or that all three had the opportunity or that all three have the means, but I truly believe that one of them did or does."

"Jericho may have a motive, I guess, to get Bob's money, but I don't see that he had any opportunity or means," said Marjorie.

"That we know of yet," cautioned Essie.

"And Violet may have a motive, but we're not sure. She had the opportunity and possibly the means, but again we're not sure," added Opal.

"Now Sue," said Essie, completing their list.  "As far as we know, she has no motive, but she had the best opportunity and possibly the means—if this dollar bill proves to be poisoned."

"Now, Essie," said Marjorie as the three women stood head to head behind their walkers outside the public restrooms at the botanical gardens.  "The question is how to find out if the dollar bill in Sue's purse is poisoned or not."

Essie also added a fourth possible suspect in her mind—Evelyn Cudahy.  As Bob's new wife, she stood to inherit all of Bob's millions—if Bob died.  Even so, Essie had promised not to reveal Bob and Evelyn's marital status and she intended to keep her word—even going so far as keeping it from her two best friends.  However, if facts developed that indicated that Evelyn was somehow implicated in Bob's recent collapse—then all promises were cancelled and all bets were off.

As Essie glanced over her shoulder and down the incline back to where the Happy Haven bus was parked, she noticed that Sue Barber was standing before the bus's door.  Sue was staring up the hill at the three elderly residents who were chatting in an animated fashion about possible attempted murder.  Did Sue realize what they suspected?  Did she notice that someone had rifled through her purse?  Essie didn't know but she had no intention of giving one of their suspects something to worry about.

"Ladies," said Essie, "We'd better go enjoy the beautiful Reardon Botanical Gardens before Sue Barber comes up this monster hill and starts asking questions."  She glanced over and smiled benignly at their Social Director.  Opal and Marjorie followed suit and soon the three women had rolled their walkers onto a path that took them into the depths of the gardens.

## Chapter Twenty-seven

*"Though an old man I am but a young gardener."*
—Thomas Jefferson

It was like a safari. Essie led Marjorie and Opal up and down the narrow paths that wound around throughout what appeared—to Essie's eyes—like some tropical jungle, not botanical gardens. As they wheeled their walkers deeper and deeper into the gardens, the branches hanging down brushed against their faces as they walked. As it was spring, many of the trees were in full bloom and sweet-smelling petals fluttered from above, landing on their hair and their walkers like confetti.

"Isn't this beautiful, Essie?" asked Marjorie, grabbing at some of the blooms and sniffing them deeply.

"Like magnolias," noted Essie, "but larger blossoms."

"All these petals are sticking to my glasses," whined Opal. "I can barely see because the branches are so thick, the sun can't even shine through."

"I know," agreed Marjorie, "it's like some tropical jungle."

"And right here in the center of our little town," added Essie. "I can't believe I've never been here before."

"You were so worried about finding a restroom," noted Marjorie.

"We did find one," said Opal.

"If you can call it that," sneered Essie. "Oh well, it was worth it. My sweet barleycorn, look over there!" She pointed to her left. In the distance, a small waterfall could be seen crashing into a flower-covered pool.

"What kind of plants are those, flower expert?" Opal asked.

"I wish I knew," answered Essie. "Most of them seem tropical. Look at the pinks and oranges."

"As much as I enjoy it here," said Marjorie, "I'm getting kind of worried about this path."

"Yes," agreed Opal, "it's really narrow and it's getting bumpy. My walker is getting stuck on all these little rocks."

"Oh my begonias," sputtered Essie, looking at her watch, "look at the time. It's almost three o'clock. We were supposed to be back at the bus at three. We'd better turn around and go back."

"Wouldn't that be the long way?" asked Marjorie. "Wouldn't we be better off going straight ahead? Surely we'll find a different path that will take us to the entrance."

"I don't know, Marjorie," said Opal, shaking her head. "The signs here all just point one direction. I think Essie is right. I think we'd better turn around and go back."

"What time is it?" asked Marjorie.

"Ten till three," said Essie, starting to turn her walker around on the bumpy  gravel pathway.

"We'll never get there in time!" cried Marjorie.

"They're not going to leave without us!" noted Opal.

"Come on, you two," said Essie, charging back the way they came with a huge shove to her walker. She stormed down the rocky winding path as fast as her spindly legs would move. Opal and Marjorie rotated their walkers and then headed after her in hot pursuit—at least as hot a pursuit as two little old ladies with walkers could do.

Essie bounded ahead with Opal and Marjorie pulling up the rear almost out of sight. As she scurried over the little road, all of a sudden a large branch fell from high up in the tops of the trees and landed immediately behind her on the pathway.

"Oh jumping Juniper tree!" she yelled as she turned to see the giant tree limb directly behind her on the ground. *If I hadn't been quite as fast as I am, it would have landed right on my head*, she thought to herself. Almost immediately, Opal and Marjorie arrived and stopped their walkers short.

"Essie!" shrieked Marjorie. "That big branch almost landed on top of you!"

"It just missed you by a few inches!" added Opal.

"You are so lucky!" said Marjorie.

"So I am," agreed Essie, breathing deeply as she surveyed the branch that had just narrowly missed smashing her to smithereens. She looked up into the trees trying to determine the source of the fallen branch. Nothing moved. *How did that happen?* she wondered. She thought that if a branch that large fell off of a tree, its source would surely be noticeable. But all the trees looked normal; none of them showed any signs of recent breakage.

"Are you okay, Essie?" asked Opal.

"Fine," responded Essie, "just a bit mystified."

"What?" asked Marjorie. "It was a fluke accident. You were lucky you were moving so fast."

"Was it a fluke?" wondered Essie out loud, staring upwards and then off into the bushes on either side of the pathway. Just where had that branch come from? Did it really fall from the trees above? Or did someone throw it onto the trail directly into Essie's pathway? She had been concentrating so hard on moving forward and getting back to the bus that she really hadn't been paying much attention to her surroundings. Not a very wise thing to do, when she was smack in the middle of investigating a possible attempted murder.

"If you're not hurt, Essie," said Opal, "maybe we should get moving. Are you able to walk?"

"Oh, I'm more than able to walk," said Essie, "No tree branch is going to get in my way."

"That's the Essie I know," said Marjorie. She and Opal moved into formation behind their leader. Essie set forth on the winding trail leading out of the botanical gardens' interior back to the entrance. After a few minutes of heavy wheeling, the three women arrived on the scene of the bus. Sue Barber was standing in front of the bus, tapping her finger on her clipboard, looking down at the sign-up sheet. As the three friends climbed aboard the bus— relegating their walkers again to the luggage compartment where the driver and Sue stored them—they were greeted by the catcalls of their fellow residents.

"Hey, Essie," said one woman, "you get lost out in the little garden?" She laughed and nudged her seatmate in the ribs.

"Essie," said a pleasant gentleman in the second row, "you're just an explorer like me. Here, have a seat." He patted the place next to him.

Essie smiled at her friends but continued to the back with Opal and Marjorie in tow.

"Have you been waiting long?" she asked.

"Nah," said one rather plump man near the rear. "Sue finally got tired of waiting for you a little after three so she went looking for you. But she came back—just shortly before the three of you showed up just now."

"Really?" asked Essie.

"Yeah," he replied. "She said she couldn't find you. She was really getting worried. I think she was about ready to contact the head of the gardens or the police or someone—then all of a sudden the three of you show up! Great timing!" He laughed and Essie and her two friends laughed too.

The three women returned to their seats at the very back of the bus.

"So," whispered Essie to her pals as the bus took off with a jerk, "Sue Barber came looking for us. Probably about the time that big branch almost splattered me into a zillion pieces."

"Essie," responded Marjorie in a hushed voice. "You don't think Sue had anything to do with that branch falling near you."

"You mean, nearly on me!" retorted Essie.

"Surely you don't think Sue tried to kill you, Essie," whispered Opal into Essie's other ear.

"I think somebody did," said Essie between her teeth, "and I intend to find out who."

## Chapter Twenty-eight

*"Does age poison us, or do we poison age?"*
—Astrid Alauda

If Sue Barber had tried to kill her at the Reardon Botanical Gardens, reasoned Essie, she probably wouldn't give up, just because her first attempt had failed. Essie figured she'd probably be safe during the day when she was around other residents. Sue wouldn't be likely to try something in front of witnesses. No, thought Essie, the dangerous time would be at night when she was asleep. She didn't lock her front door—no one did because aides and staff members had to be able to get into apartments to assist residents who might need help. Locked doors just slowed them down and increased the chances that falls and sudden illnesses could not be dealt with in a timely fashion.

But, now after the episode in the gardens with the large branch, she worried that as soon as she fell asleep, Sue Barber would sneak into her room and finish her off. It would be easy to do and probably no one would be the wiser. Sue would just probably wait until late and then come into Essie's bedroom and smother her with a pillow.

*Wait a minute*, Essie told herself. If it was so easy to murder a resident in their room, why hadn't Sue just done that to Bob Weiderley? Why go through all the rigmarole of killing him with a poisoned dollar bill at Bingo? It seemed excessively convoluted. It wasn't as if Bob could fight her off if she decided to strangle him in his bed. And why would Sue want to kill Bob anyway? Or her?

It was now late afternoon and Essie was doing her contemplating in her comfortable arm chair in her living room. Marjorie and Opal had returned to their rooms too. All three women were exhausted—not only from the hiking and walking they'd done at the botanical gardens, but from the excitement and fear they had experienced with Essie's close call with the branch—and ultimately their suspicion that Sue Barber had caused the debacle.

Essie picked up her clipboard from her end table and aimlessly began filling in boxes in her crossword puzzle of the day. The definition for fourteen across was "hired killer." *So much for helping get my mind off my problems*, she thought as she wrote in "assassin" in the spaces.

There was a knock at her door. Essie almost jumped out of her chair she was so on edge. Surely, it wasn't Sue Barber come round to finish the job. She wouldn't risk it right in the middle of the afternoon with so many residents walking around.

"Who's there?" she called out, moving as quickly as possible from her chair and grabbing a large serving spoon from the top drawer in her kitchen nook. She clung to the front door knob when there was no answer.

"Who's there?" she called out again through the crack between the door and the door frame. No response. Now, this is ridiculous. A murderer doesn't knock on the door and then say nothing. Slowly she turned the knob and ever so cautiously peeked around the corner.

"Stars' bars!" she exclaimed. "Fay, what are you doing here?" Sweet, plump and generally silent Fay sat in her wheelchair in the hallway, her hands folded discreetly in her lap and resting on a pile of papers. Fay smiled at Essie.

"I didn't even know that you knew which room I was in," said Essie. "Do you want to come in?" she asked her quiet, sleepy tablemate. Fay said nothing but handed Essie the pile of papers in her lap. Essie glanced down and noticed that she was looking at more print-outs from the family room computer—possibly a good thirty or forty pages.

"What's all this?" asked Essie.

"Poison," said Fay succinctly. Then wheeling herself around, she headed back down the hallway.

"Thank you, Fay," yelled Essie after her. Essie shut her door, stopping only to ponder whether or not it might be possible to devise some sort of lock for her front door that would prevent Sue Barber from entering but not to prevent her aides from entering should she need their help in the middle of the night. There didn't seem to be any way.

She rolled herself back to her chair, parked her walker, and plopped back down so she could examine the material that Fay had brought her. Quickly, she thumbed through the stack. There were sections from encyclopedias and medical reference books. There were what appeared to be question and answer sites for patients to ask doctors questions about their symptoms. There were photographs. There were quotations from quite a number of murder mysteries by different authors. Fay had evidently gone through some of the material and marked certain lines and paragraphs with a pen. *My goodness*, thought Essie, *that sweet lady that we always consider only about half there most of the time, seems to have the research skills of a trained librarian.* Essie couldn't remember what Fay had done before she retired, but surely it must have been something that involved searching for information because it was quite evident that she was very good at it.

Now, the question was whether or not all of this information would be of any help in trying to determine if Sue Barber or someone else poisoned Bob Weiderley. Evelyn Cudahy (or rather Evelyn Weiderley) had told her that the doctors had found some strange substance in Bob's bloodstream and Essie suspected that that substance was poison. Essie plumped the pages together neatly into their original order. Starting with the first page, she began to read. The first sections concerned poisons in general— what technically constituted a poison from a medical and a legal standpoint. There were categories for different types of poisons. One category system of great interest to her was based on how a poison is delivered into the body. Obviously, the most commonly used method in most murder mysteries was by mouth. However, poisons could also be absorbed, she read, by inhalation and through the skin.

She thought about the dollar bill she had found in Sue Barber's purse. It was in a plastic bag. Why? Was it because it was drenched in poison and Sue Barber wanted to avoid contact with it or prevent anyone else from having contact with it? If that was the case, she wondered, why didn't Sue just get rid of it? She could cut it up—no, it would still be poisonous whether or not it was in small pieces. What if she burned it in a fire? Would the fumes be poisonous? She didn't know. And if that dollar was poisonous, how did Sue hand it to Bob for the Bingo prize (which she did) without herself getting poisoned? Did she protect herself in some way? Was it because she was younger and stronger than Bob? That sounded a little risky to Essie. She surely wouldn't risk poisoning someone by handing them some poisoned substance and just hope it didn't poison her too.

She continued reading. There was information on poison strength. Some poisons were lethal in extremely small amounts— others required that larger quantities be consumed or ingested in some way before they became toxic. Some poisons acted immediately; others took quite some time to take effect. Some poisons were cumulative; others were not. That is, one type of poison would be secreted from the body quickly so that a second dose would be no more lethal than the first. A second type of poison might remain in the body for a long time so that a second dose would combine with that already present and form a lethal combination.

After she completed reading the entire stack of information—at least a quick reading, if not a thorough one—she felt that she understood HOW Sue Barber might have poisoned Bob Weiderley and possibly with what type of poison. What she didn't know was WHY. The same held true for Violet Hendrickson. It was possible that Violet had been able to devise some sort of poison delivery system to dose Bob, but less likely. Violet, however, as Essie saw it, had a possible motive. Bob was apparently aware of her criminal record (if the newspaper clipping she'd found under the desk blotter in his apartment was any indication) and Violet was the Director of Happy Haven which would benefit greatly in a financial sense if Bob died (at least if he died before he changed his will to leave his wealth to his new wife Evelyn). But Bob and Sue had no adversarial relationship. Why would Sue want to poison Bob? Sue didn't benefit from Bob's death, not that Essie could see anyway. There was Sue and there was Violet—one with motive and no means, and the other with means and no motive.

Essie thought and thought about the two women—the Director of Happy Haven and the Social Director. Violet was Sue's immediate superior. *Surely*, thought Essie, *it can't be that Violet ordered Sue to kill Bob Weiderley?* That just seemed too gruesome. But how was it any more gruesome than either of them deciding to kill the poor old gentleman all alone?

The two women obviously worked closely together. Their offices were side by side. Maybe they planned the murder together. Maybe they were like a team working together to wipe out old people wherever they could—especially old men who had left all of their money to the place where the two women worked.

"Residents," announced Phyllis on the intercom, "dinner is served. Time for those of you scheduled for first sitting to come get in line. The chef tells us that the pork chops are especially divine tonight!"

"Great!" said Essie. She gathered the papers and placed them on her end table, leaving the unread pages on top and at a right angle to the read pages. Then after her usual quick trip to the bathroom to straighten her hair and 'other things' she pushed her walker out into the hallway (checking both directions to make sure Sue Barber wasn't lying in wait for her as she exited) and headed off to the divine pork chops in the dining room.

### Chapter Twenty-nine

*"The age of a woman doesn't mean a thing.  The best tunes are played on the oldest fiddles."*
—Ralph Waldo Emerson

In the middle of their divine pork chops, the women considered their exploits that afternoon in the botanical gardens.  They were still frightened and worried about Essie's near brush with death.  Just how, they wondered, did that large branch barely miss her?  They told Fay about their adventures but Fay seemed oblivious to their tale.  Essie wondered.

"Fay found quite a bit of interesting information about poison," she whispered to Opal and Marjorie.  Marjorie took a more scrutinizing look at her pork chop and Opal pushed her plate away.

"Essie," chided Opal, "you really know how to kill a person's appetite.  Do we have to discuss poison at the dinner table?"

"I just thought you'd like to know about all the research Fay did while we were out gallivanting around in Mother Nature."

"You mean while you were out getting practically smashed by a huge tree limb!" exclaimed Marjorie.  Fay remained unmoved as she continued to nibble on her divine chop.

"Keep your voice down," hushed Essie.  "Sue and Violet are still in the dining room.  They might overhear us."

"They're all the way over by the window," noted Opal.  "They don't have super hearing."

"You know," suggested Essie, looking back and forth from one friend to another, "if Sue and Violet are here eating dinner, you know what that means?"

"That they're not poisoning anyone?" asked Opal with a sneer.

"No!" said Essie with a curt nod to Opal.  "It means they're not in their offices."

"So?" said Marjorie, tentatively returning to her pork chop.

"I'm thinking," said Essie, "that maybe we could slip out before they leave here, and just happen by their offices."

"Why?" asked Marjorie.

"Maybe we could find a clue," said Essie with a sway of her shoulders.

"Such as what?" asked Opal.  "An incriminating giant box of poison?"

Santos, who was working the dinner shift tonight in addition to his regular day shift, arrived with the desserts the women had ordered and proceeded to exchange their entree plates for the smaller dessert bowls.

"Cobbler!" screamed Marjorie. "My favorite!"

"Be careful.  It might be poisoned!" said Opal.

"Oh, Miss Opal!" gasped Santos. "Never would Santos serve a dessert that would harm his favorite ladies in any way."

"No, Santos," said Essie, patting the arm of the young waiter, "Opal and Marjorie are just having a disagreement over a . . . movie they saw.  One of the characters was poisoned and they thought it was delivered in his food . . ."

"But it was in his clothing, right?" offered Santos, "I see that movie, I think, Miss Essie.  Very clever."  He continued passing the cobblers around the table.

"How did they get poison in his clothing?" asked Essie.

"I think they poured it in washer and then washed his pajamas in it.  It was safe when someone just touch the pajamas, but when man wear pajamas all night— all over his body—poison rub off during night into his skin," explained Santos as he completed his task, and wiping off a small amount of spilled tea in front of Fay's place, he headed back to the kitchen.

"What do you think of that?" asked Essie.

"You mean, did someone wash Bob's pajamas in poison?" asked Opal.  "Who would do that?   Other than his cleaning woman?  And why would she?"

*Or*, thought Essie, *maybe his wife. Someone who would know for certain what pajamas he wore—or that he wore pajamas. Oh my, the plot is just too thick.* Her head was spinning.

"So," said Essie finally, "are we going to do it?"

"Do what?" asked Marjorie.

"Look for clues in the . . . offices," replied Essie.

"Oh, will this ever end?" whined Opal, hand to her head. "Oh, all right! Let's go!" The four women rose, grabbed their walkers, and filed out of the dining hall.

"Fay," said Essie to her wheelchair-bound friend, "you'd better wait here in the lobby—or work at the computers if you like."

Fay smiled sweetly and rolled off into the family room. The remaining women rolled their walkers to the right and around the corner that led to the office wing. As they headed down the carpeted hallway, they noticed that most of the glass-enclosed offices along the left-side of the hallway were deserted. Most of the various directors of Happy Haven had probably left for the evening. Only those individuals such as Sue Barber who worked directly with residents would be likely to remain into the evenings. The financial director and publicity director and whatever other directors worked here (Essie really didn't know because most of these people she didn't know) probably kept bankers' hours.

"Where do we start?" asked Opal as the threesome halted midway down the hallway.

"I want to check out Sue's office to see if she has any poison hidden anywhere," said Essie. She rolled her walker into the office with Sue's nameplate on the glass door. "Opal, you know your job."

"I know," said Opal. "Lookout." Opal rolled her walker back around and headed down to the entrance to the office wing from the lobby. Essie rolled into Sue's office as Marjorie remained at her door where she could see both Essie and Opal just in case Essie had to move out of the office quickly.

Essie scooted around to Sue's small metal desk which was flush against a wall. Quickly she surveyed the items on top of the desk and nothing appeared unusual. She opened all of the drawers looking for a container of liquid or powder or something that might ostensibly be poison. The only thing incriminating she found was a bottle of nail polish. *She probably didn't poison Bob with this*, thought Essie.

Leaving Sue Barber's desk, Essie moved around the small room. There were several comfortable chairs and a long table against the other wall. On this table were various games, sporting equipment, assorted prizes for contests, and other paraphernalia. Under the table were stacked five or six boxes. She opened one and discovered costumes that Sue evidently intended to use or had used for a Halloween party.

Then Essie checked inside a small closet near Sue's office door. Here she found a jacket and on the floor a pair of overshoes. On the shelf above she found cleaning supplies—paper towels, rubber gloves, a bottle of cleaning spray, and a box of sponges. Apparently, if Sue had squirreled away any poison she used on Bob Weiderley, she wasn't keeping it in her office.

Essie rolled out of Sue's office with a glance at Marjorie. Marjorie nodded and indicated that Opal was at the entrance to the office wing and so far no one was coming. Essie moved on down the hallway to Violet's office. This too, like Sue's office, was unlocked. Essie opened the door and wheeled herself inside. Marjorie nodded at her and continued to keep her eye on Opal at the far end of the hallway.

Violet's office was much more daunting to explore than Sue's. Violet had been at Happy Haven longer and obviously she had accumulated much more stuff. Violet's desk sat facing the doorway with her back to the window on the opposite side. Her desk was larger than Sue's and was covered with more papers and files. Essie glanced around at the material on the desk but didn't see anything obviously incriminating. She opened all of the drawers where she found a multitude of hanging files meticulously catalogued and labeled. Along the right wall, five filing cabinets stood. Essie quickly opened all the drawers of all the cabinets. At the cabinet nearest the window, the lowest drawer would not open. Essie realized that this cabinet had a locking mechanism and that the bottom drawer was locked. *Hmmm*, she wondered. *What was so important or secret that Violet had it locked up?* She rolled back over to the desk and pulled out the center drawer which she had already searched. She remembered two small gold keys in this drawer but no indication on them as to what they were for. Grabbing both keys, she moved back to the filing cabinet near the window, bent down and slipped the little key into the cabinet lock. The key fit and turned and the lower cabinet drawer slid out with a few jerks.

Inside, Essie found virtually nothing. Nothing except a manila envelope lying on the bottom of the drawer. *What?* she wondered. She picked up the envelope and opened it. Inside, she found newspaper clippings—one that was quite familiar and several more that she hadn't seen. All detailed the criminal records of different women over about a forty year period. One woman was named Vivian Hollingsworth, one Vivica Hempstead, and a third was Violet Hendrickson. It was this third clipping she had seen in Bob Weiderley's apartment. The women in the other two articles also had DUI records just like Violet. The three women in the newspaper stories had even more in common than their criminal drinking behavior. From just a cursory glance at the accompanying photographs of the three, it was obvious that they were all Violet Hendrickson.

"Essie," called out Marjorie, "Someone's coming!"

Essie shoved the clippings back in the envelope, dropped the envelope back in the drawer, slammed the drawer shut, locked it, rumbled over to the desk and dropped the keys in. Then she quickly pushed her walker as fast as possible out through Violet's office door and she and Marjorie headed down the hallway in the opposite direction from where Opal had just signaled them that someone was coming. They pulled around a corner near the end of the hallway which dead-ended at a closet door, just as Sue and Violet sauntered down the hallway laughing and chatting. They each entered their offices.

"Now what?" whispered Marjorie to Essie as they shivered behind the small nook at the end of the hallway. Essie peeked out.

She could see Opal at the distant end. She motioned to her to come towards them. Opal cringed and shook her head. Essie continued to point, indicating Sue and Violet's offices. Finally, when nothing seemed to be happening, Opal took a deep breath and stormed her walker down the hallway, stopping directly between Sue and Violet's door. She started yelling.

"Help me, please! Help, Miss Violet! Miss Sue!" Opal carried on like crazy, screaming and calling for the two women. Violet and Sue came out of their offices and spoke to Opal. Essie and Marjorie could see them comforting her but they had no idea what crazy story Opal was feeding the two directors. After a few moments, Opal's legs seemed to give way and Sue and Violet escorted her into Violet's office where they all three disappeared. At that moment, Essie wheeled her walker down the hallway as fast as she could.

"Come on, Marjorie," she whispered to her friend right behind her. As they closed in on Sue's office they peeked through the glass wall where they saw Opal seated in one of Sue's comfortable chairs and Sue and Violet kneeling before her. Opal noticed Essie and Marjorie pass by all the while she continued to moan about some mysterious ailment. When Essie and Marjorie arrived in the lobby, they checked first to make certain that their appearance from the office wing would not be noticed and then when it was clear, they rolled into the lobby and quickly took up positions on a lobby sofa that was positioned so that they could see anyone exiting the office wing.

In a few minutes, Opal appeared at the entrance to the office wing. Sue and Violet were on either side of her being very solicitous.

"No, no," said Opal to Sue and Violet, "I'm really fine now. I don't know what came over me. It must have been that cobbler. It just didn't set right with me for some reason. I usually just love it! You don't need to stay with me. I'm really just fine!" Opal smiled heroically at the two directors who retreated squeamishly back into the office wing. As soon as they were out of sight, Essie and

Marjorie, bounded up from their seats and rolled quickly over to Opal.

"Opal," said Essie, hugging her lanky friend with joy, "You are my hero!"

"Mine too!" agreed Marjorie, giving Opal a super tight squeeze.

"It was nothing," shrugged Opal, "just a little bit of light acting."

They all laughed and headed off to the family room to find Fay.

## Chapter Thirty

*"Men do not quit playing because they grow old; they grow old because they quit playing."*
—Oliver Wendell Holmes

Later that night, after she had enjoyed her weekly shower and had settled to watch one of those ubiquitous reality television shows from the comfort of her soft armchair and her flannel nightie, Essie was able to think back on what had turned out to be a rather extraordinary day.  The botanical gardens in the afternoon and then the search of the directors' offices and the close call when she and Marjorie were almost caught in their espionage.  It made Essie smile to think that she could accomplish so much at her advanced age.  She resolved never to let her age be a hindrance in doing what she wanted to do.  She'd rather go out with a bang than a whimper, as that W. C. Fields always used to say.

The phone startled her from her thoughts.  Who in the world would be calling her so late at night?  It was after eight o'clock and people should be heading to bed, she reasoned.  She quickly answered the phone, worried that one of her three children or one of their children might be sick or injured.

"Miss Cobb," said the voice of a man.  "Miss Cobb?  I don't know if you'll remember me, but we spoke in your lobby a few days ago.  I'm Ben Jericho.  I've been looking for Mr. Weiderley—Mr. Bob Weiderley.  Do you remember talking to me?  When I was there, your Director, Miss Hendrickson, told me he was on a fishing trip and she didn't know when he'd return."

"Oh, Mr. Jericho," said Essie, surprised.  "I didn't expect to hear from you."

"Yes," he replied, "I suppose you didn't. Actually, I just called your front desk to see if Mr. Weiderley had returned and the clerk said he hadn't. I asked if I could speak to you so they rang your apartment. I'm sorry for calling so late."

"I was getting ready for bed," she stammered. "I . . . I'm really very . . . tired."

"I'm so sorry, Miss Cobb . . . Miss Essie, if I may call you that. You were so kind to speak to me the other day. I won't keep you long."

"All right," she agreed, cautiously. "But I really can't talk long."

"Of course," he replied. "I only wanted to ask you if you had heard from Bob—Mr. Weiderley. Maybe, I was thinking, he might have contacted you or one of his friends at Happy Haven to let them know when he's returning. I'm really very anxious to contact him."

"So you said, Mr. Jericho," responded Essie, "but Mr. Jericho, I'm not in a position to discuss Bob's, Mr. Weiderley's whereabouts with someone I don't really know. I mean, I have only your word that you know him. I've never heard Bob, Mr. Weiderley, say anything about you. For all I know, you might be trying to fleece him. I mean, he is an old man. Sometimes, people do try to scam old people like us." She was quite proud of the argument she had just presented on the spur of the moment. She felt she had indicated why she had reservations about providing Jericho with any pertinent information about Bob without actually revealing anything she shouldn't.

"I see," responded Jericho, quietly. There was a fairly long pause as the man appeared to be contemplating his next move. *Or maybe*, thought, Essie, *he is devising how he'll have to revise his scheme so he can scam both of us now.*

"Miss Essie," said Jericho finally, "I don't suppose Mr. Weiderley ever told you about me, did he?"

"No, Mr. Jericho, I believe I can safely say that he didn't." She didn't add that she, however, had rummaged through Bob's apartment and discovered the letter that he had sent to Bob

claiming to be his long lost illegitimate son. "Although . . . —"
She stopped herself.

"Yes, Miss Essie?" he asked.

"Although I was curious about you and your business when you
gave me your card," she said. "I even asked my doctor if she had
heard of you—I mean if she'd heard of your company."

"And had she?"

"It appears that your Medilogi—whatever it is, is quite well-
known among physicians."

"That's gratifying to hear. I hope your doctor didn't have
anything bad to say about us."

"No," said Essie. "Quite the contrary. She sang your praises
and said you were sort of the—now who was that man she
compared you to? Oh, she said you were. . . I know—the Donald
Trump of medical softeners."

"She probably meant software," he corrected gently, "and—
wow! No one has ever compared me to the Donald before."

"Does that mean that you own a lot of buildings, Mr. Jericho?"
asked Essie.

"My goodness, Miss Essie," he said laughing, "here I thought I
was interrogating you!"

"You were, Mr. Jericho?"

"You know, Miss Essie," he said, "can I be frank?"

"I really wish you would, Mr. Jericho," answered Essie, "it
might save us all a lot of time."

"It's quite evident to me that you are one smart lady."

"I already know that," she responded with a vocal shrug.

"I think you know exactly where Bob Weiderley is, don't you?"

"Why do you say that?" she questioned. *Now why*, she
wondered *was he doubting her?*.

"I can't imagine you'd bother to investigate me and my
company if you had absolutely no interest in this situation, which
suggests to me that you know where Mr. Weiderley is—or at least
you know something about his absence. You must have some
strong reason for not wanting me to contact him."

"I already told you. I'm not at liberty to discuss Bob's situation with you. I have no authority to do so. It's not like Bob told me to communicate with you or to tell you where he is."

"Then you do know where he is?"

"Fishing."

"No, where he really is," said Jericho firmly.

"Mr. Jericho," replied Essie, "you're a very charming and persuasive man, but I wouldn't tell you where Bob Weiderley is— if I knew—and I don't. So that's all there is to it." Essie crossed her fingers as she told this whopper of a lie to the man.

"I only wish you could give me a clue—or a little hope, Miss Essie," he pleaded. "Truly, I have nowhere else to turn. I'm not trying to hurt Mr. Weiderley. I wish you could believe me."

"I wish I could too, Mr. Jericho," she said. "Maybe he'll return from his fishing trip—soon. You never know."

"You do know something!" he cried. "Did he call you? Did he call someone there? Is he scheduled to return to Happy Haven? Can't you please give me a hint? It's not as if I can do anything to him."

"I don't know that, Mr. Jericho."

"You have my sworn word, Miss Essie."

"And what are you swearing on, Mr. Jericho?" she asked.

"What do you want me to swear on?" he asked.

"How about your father's life?" she sputtered out.

Jericho was silent for a few moments, and then he spoke quietly.

"Miss Essie," he said slowly, "I don't know . . . exactly what you're trying to say . . . but I'm going to guess . . . hope . . . that you're sending me a message of encouragement. I'm going to hope that you're suggesting that I return to Happy Haven and try to speak with Bob."

"You can read into my remarks what you will, Mr. Jericho," she replied.

"I don't know what you know, or think you know, Miss Essie," he said carefully, "but whatever it is, there is nothing about my intentions that Mr. Weiderley needs to fear. Please believe me."

"On your father's life, Mr. Jericho," she repeated.

"On my father's life," he agreed. "Good night, Miss Essie. I'm sorry I kept you up so late. Sleep tight. Good bye."

"Good bye, Mr. Jericho," she responded and hung up the phone.

*Very interesting*, she said to herself. She had learned more about the mysterious Ben Jericho and the company for which he worked. The man had not—and apparently would not—reveal to her his supposed biological relationship with Bob Weiderley—if there was such a relationship. There was no way for her to know if Bob was actually this man's father until and unless she was able to ask Bob himself. Bob obviously had read Jericho's letter and it probably had upset him. What Essie didn't know is if Bob was upset because the information in Jericho's letter was true and Bob was shocked to find out he had a son or because it was false and he was petrified that Jericho was trying to scam him. Essie's feelings in the matter vacillated back and forth. Even so, it didn't matter how Essie felt because it was up to Bob to decide whether or not he wished to contact or be contacted by Ben Jericho—and Bob could hardly do that from his hospital bed. She—and Jericho— would just have to wait until Bob returned from his—fishing trip. She had hinted that Bob might be returning soon and that was as far as she could ethically go, she believed. The next move was Jericho's.

Essie shimmied out of her deep, soft chair and wheeled her walker into her bedroom. Slipping out of her robe which she deposited across the top of her trusty vehicle (in case she had to make a late night trip to the potty, she didn't want to freeze) and slipping off her slippers beside her bed, she crawled under her sheets and her toasty warm, peach-colored duvet. As she had a clean conscience (always a wonderful soporific), she was sound asleep in just a few moments.

## Chapter Thirty-one

*"In a dream you are never eighty."*
—Anne Sexton

Essie's dreams of skipping through a flower-covered botanical garden without the help of a walker were interrupted with a start when she heard the sound of her apartment door creaking open. Essie sat up in bed, thinking to herself that it was probably Sue Barber come to finish her off since she hadn't been able to smash her that afternoon with the tree limb.  Or maybe it was Violet, who had seen her burglarize her office and discover the incriminating newspaper clippings that revealed her multiple identities, now arriving in the dead of night to smother her with a pillow.  Oh, why didn't she prop a chair under her front door knob like they did in the movies to keep the gangsters out?  Now she had just seconds to live before the unknown murderer ended her fragile life with ease. She cringed under the covers, shaking, trying to think how she could defend herself.  Was there anything here in her bedroom she could use to knock the culprit on the noggin as she came near? What could she use?  Her lamp?  Too big and plugged in?  She had a pile of books stacked on her bedside but they were all fairly small and would probably only make a small knot on the fiend's forehead.  Jumping Jezebels!  What could she do?

As she shook in contemplation, Fay's head poked around her bedroom door.

"Fay!" whispered Essie in relief when she saw that her quiet friend was the one guilty of breaking and entering and not Sue Barber or Violet Hendrickson.  "Why are you roaming around in the middle of the night? "

Fay wheeled her wheelchair carefully into Essie's bedroom, maneuvering skillfully around the door jamb and closer to Essie's bed.  She pointed at her wristwatch.

Essie glanced over at her bedside alarm clock.

"Oh," she said, deflated, "it's only 10:30.  I guess it's not that late.  But still, Fay!  Why didn't you knock?  You scared me to death!"

Fay hung her head and looked sad.  Finally, she squeaked, "Sorry."  Then she reached inside a side pocket of her wheelchair and brought out some more computer print-outs.

"More computer research, Fay!" cried Essie.  "Couldn't this have waited until morning?"

Fay pointed at the pages which Essie really couldn't see well in the faint moonlight streaming into her bedroom.  She reached over and turned on her bedside table lamp.  A blast of light filled the room.  Both women squinted.  Essie reached out and took the small pile of paper as Fay remained in her wheelchair watching.

"New clues?" she asked Fay.  "Is this about Violet or Sue?  Or maybe Ben Jericho?  You've been doing great finding all this information, Fay.  I had no idea you knew so much about computers."

"Librarian," said Fay cautiously and with difficulty.

"You were a librarian?" asked Essie.

Fay nodded. "Son," she added.

"Your son is a librarian? Or he taught you to use computers?  Oh, well, I guess it doesn't matter."  She grabbed her glasses from her table and slipped them over her ears so she could read the small print on the pages.

"Hmm," she muttered as she perused the first page.  "This isn't about . . . oh my, Fay!  This is about John!  My husband!  How did you . . .?  Oh, look, I've never read this before.  It's a tribute someone wrote about him after he . . . died.  I thought I'd seen everything that was written about him; people sent me these articles in newspapers, but this is . . . this is lovely.  Oh, Fay.  Where did you find this?"  She continued reading, her eyes filling with tears.  Fay watched and waited.  Eventually, Essie looked up.

She grabbed a tissue from the dispenser on her nightstand and wiped her eyes. "Thank you for bringing me this."

Fay pointed to the second page. Essie glanced down and began to read. This page was also a tribute, but it was in honor of Opal's husband, Fred. Essie finished reading and smiled at Fay. Fay handed her another page and—not unexpectedly, another tribute, this time to Marjorie's deceased spouse, Albert. With one page left, Essie reached out and took the page. This tribute, so similar to those of the other three husbands was devoted to the memory of Fay's Michael. Essie read this one out loud and with great tenderness. As she read, she watched Fay who listened and smiled—and eventually sobbed as Essie described the wonderful qualities of a man whom Fay had obviously adored—but whom she obviously was unable to discuss herself. When Essie had finished reading the tribute to Fay's husband, Fay grabbed Essie's hands, squeezed them, and quickly brought them to her lips and kissed them sweetly.

"Thank you, Fay," whispered Essie. "Thank you for sharing these eulogies with me. It makes me feel so much closer to you and Marjorie and Opal, knowing more about all of your husbands. It's a wonderful bond between us. Thank you for bringing these to me. Should we share them with Marjorie and Opal?"

Fay nodded and reached out and hugged Essie. Then smiling, she wheeled her chair backwards and around the bedroom door jamb and out of Essie's apartment. Essie could hear the front door latch shut. She had thought of Fay as a strange little woman, sort of a tagalong to their group. She hardly spoke; she slept more often than not, yet she had amazing skills when she put her mind to it. The information she had extracted from her computer searches were proof of that. Now, this middle of the night visit was another indication of Fay's unique and strange persona. Essie didn't know quite what to make of Fay—maybe she would never know. But she did know that Fay was a good friend and that she would not ever again take her for granted.

## Chapter Thirty-two

*"It's sad to grow old, but nice to ripen."*
—Brigitte Bardot

Essie made it through the rest of the night with no further break-ins. No one attempted to murder her. She also made it through breakfast without being poisoned—at least she had so far. Although, the blueberry pancakes did have a strange wood-like quality. True to her word, Fay brought the tributes to their husbands that she had found on the computer and shared them with Opal and Marjorie. Opal had seen the one for Fred before in her local newspaper, but for Marjorie the article on her husband Albert was totally new and all four women shared her joy in reading someone else's homage to the most important person in Marjorie's life. In truth, thought Essie, this was certainly one of the most wonderful breakfasts the four women had shared. All three of the walker users assisted the wheelchair user—Fay—in exiting the dining hall where they congregated in the lobby chatting and socializing with other residents. As they stood there, someone said:

"Look, it's Bob Weiderley!"

And everyone in the lobby looked towards the main entrance door to discover Bob Weiderley, looking a bit paler than usual, entering the building. He was accompanied by Evelyn Cudahy at his side, assisting him. As he walked through the door, leaning on his cane, a cheer went up from the entire group of residents gathered in the lobby. Bob smiled and looked at Evelyn who also smiled. Bob raised his hand and acknowledged his fellow Happy Haveners. Essie, Marjorie, and Opal stood to the side in rapt attention as Bob moved into the lobby.

"Sit down, Bob!" yelled one of his Canasta buddies.  All of the residents shouted their agreement to this request and Bob cautiously limped over to the centrally located sofa and eased himself down into the cushions, still holding firmly to his cane. Evelyn sat beside him, continuing to clutch his sleeve.

"I didn't expect such a great welcome back!" said Bob, smiling pointedly all around to everyone.

The noise of all the cheering seemed to bring out more people to see what all the noise was.  Staff members came in from the dining hall and from out of the hallways.  Phyllis stood at the front counter, beaming at the action.   Violet Hendrickson and Sue Barber appeared from the office wing and stood at its entrance watching Bob's homecoming.   Hazel Brubaker and Rose Lane watched from near the elevator.

"Bob," yelled another man standing behind him, "whatever happened at Bingo?   You really hit the floor!   Too much excitement in winning that big prize, eh?"

"Must have been," agreed Bob, smiling.  Essie wondered at his response.  Was this a politically expedient remark?  Was Bob being polite or did he suspect someone had poisoned him?  Or was he really excited at winning Bingo?  Or was he excited or nervous about something else?  Like a scam artist or possible illegitimate son?  Would Bob open up about what happened to him now here in the lobby in front of everyone or would they have to wait until later—if at all—to find out the truth?

"Are you feeling better, Bob?" asked a tiny lady to Bob's right.

"Better than ever," noted Bob.

"Do they know what caused you to collapse?" asked another.

"They . . . uh . . . found a substance in my bloodstream," replied Bob, tentatively.

"Not marijuana?" suggested a big, round man, laughing.

"Naw," laughed Bob.

"Was it poison?" asked Essie, suddenly.  She felt foolish immediately for jumping the gun—and possibly revealing her cards too soon.  She surely didn't want to upset Bob just when he had come back.

"Naw," laughed Bob. "At least not poison for most people."

"What do you mean?" asked Essie. She glanced over to Sue Barber to see if she was indicating any concern over the topic of this discussion. Sue looked concerned but not particularly worried.

"Actually, it's rather embarrassing," continued Bob.

"All the more reason to tell us," egged the fat man.

Bob chuckled. "I suppose you people will never leave me alone until I tell you, will you?

"Right you are, Steeve-arino!" said another man. Essie thought the men at Happy Haven were certainly enjoying Bob's discomfort. The women seemed more concerned about his health and welfare.

"I suppose before I explain, I should—that is, we should make another announcement," said Bob looking at Evelyn. She nodded at him, blushing. The crowd had now grown to include, in Essie's estimation, practically everyone who lived and worked at Happy Haven. *Who was manning the wheel?* she wondered, *if there was a wheel.*

"Two weeks ago," said Bob, "I asked Miss Cudahy here if she would honor me by becoming my wife. I was astounded when she agreed."

"No wonder you collapsed!" said fat man. "I would too if I could sweet talk a babe like Evelyn into marrying me!"

"We were married a week and a half ago at city hall," continued Bob. Gasps and applause were the response to this announcement. Bob took Evelyn's hand and squeezed it. They looked at each other with obvious joy. Hazel and Rose beamed from beside the elevator with nary a sign of a shake from Hazel or a tear from Rose.

Phyllis, at the front desk, grabbed her intercom microphone and said: "Residents, I have a wonderful announcement! Bob Weiderley and Evelyn Cudahy are married!"

"Phyllis," said a woman standing near the front desk. "Who's listening to their intercom? Everyone in the building is standing here in the lobby." Everyone laughed.

"Okay, okay," continued another man, "so you two got married. Is that why you collapsed? You said a strange substance was in your bloodstream?"

"It's rather embarrassing," noted Bob, clutching his cane and looking at the floor and then at his wife. "I am 86 and well, I've never been married before. I wasn't exactly certain how . . . if . . . —"

"I told him not to worry," said Evelyn sweetly, staring into Bob's eyes. "I told him nothing mattered except that we loved each other."

*Boy*, thought Essie to herself, *if Evelyn married Bob for his money, she sure isn't acting like it. It looks like she really cares about the guy. Of course, you never know.*

"Anyway," continued Bob, "I decided before the wedding to try to insure that our honeymoon which was actually just our wedding night in my apartment here . . ."

*Must have been the time Bev the beautician had seen the couple head into the elevator together all gooey-eyed*, surmised Essie.

"I decided to try this herbal powder that I'd seen advertised in a magazine. I ordered some and had started to use it—and actually I thought it was working pretty good . . ."

"So did I!" agreed Evelyn with a coy smile.

"But that's what the doctors found in my bloodstream. This weird herb." *And that Marjorie had discovered in Bob's medicine cabinet*, thought Essie.

"Is that what caused you to collapse, Bob?" asked Essie, now wondering how this information affected her concern that Sue Barber had attempted to kill Bob with a poison-drenched dollar bill.

"Nope," said Bob. "My physicians think this herb I was taking might have interacted with one of my prescription drugs."

"Did they find any other substances in your blood?" asked Essie.

"You're really probing, Essie," said Bob.

"She's been really concerned about you, dear," said Evelyn softly to her husband. "And she's been very good to me while you were in the hospital."

"Then, no, Essie. They didn't find anything else." Bob smiled at Essie who continued to look befuddled as she glanced back at Sue Barber.

"Then they don't have any idea why you collapsed?" she asked. "I mean, you yelled 'Bingo' and Miss Barber checked your tiles and you had all the correct ones. Then she handed you the dollar bill for winning and then you collapsed."

"Actually, Essie," said Bob, "you're wrong. Miss Barber did hold out the dollar bill to me, but I never got it. I was on the floor before I could even get my prize!"

"I can remedy that," offered Sue Barber, from the sidelines, coming forward and reaching into her purse. "After the EMTs took you away, Bob, I put your winning dollar bill in a plastic bag and stuck it in my purse for safe keeping and to keep it separate from my own money. I figured you'd want your prize when you returned!"

"You're right, Miss Barber!" said Bob with enthusiasm. "Give me that huge prize I won so I can hand it over to the ol' ball and chain." He smiled sweetly at Evelyn and she gave him a nudge in the ribs. Sue Barber took the dollar out of the plastic bag and handed it to Bob.

Essie cringed. Was it really safe for Bob to handle? Surely, if it wasn't, Sue wouldn't be showing it off so publicly. If Bob collapsed again and poison was discovered in his system, everyone would suspect immediately that it came from Sue's dollar bill.

"The final diagnosis," said Bob, "is that the doctors don't really know why I collapsed. Isn't that the way it usually is? They said it was no doubt stress. Ha! I guess you might consider getting married and trying to have a successful honeymoon—all in secret—stressful." He and Evelyn smiled at each other again.

"But, Bob," called out the fat friend, "why'd you have to keep your marriage a secret?"

"We just didn't want anyone to make a fuss," he offered, "and with Evelyn going through all this chemo . . ."

"Bob wanted to keep everything low-key," said Evelyn, "but I tried to tell him that happy stress wouldn't bother me.  The stress that bothered me was him being in the coma.  But, he's better now, so I'm feeling much better."

"And she's doing much better too," said Bob to the crowd. Everyone responded with happy sounds.

"Looks like it all worked out for the best!" cried out another woman from far across the room.

"Yes, it did!" agreed Bob, reaching over and giving his new bride a big kiss.  The crowd screamed and clapped enthusiastically. Then, as it was evident that the show was over, most started to return to their previous activities.  As they dispersed, Evelyn looked up and called to Essie.

"Essie," she said.  "I appreciate all of your kind support for me while Bob was in the hospital."

"And I appreciate it too, Essie," added Bob leaning forward. Essie sat down across from the happy couple.  Fay, Opal, and Marjorie moved closer behind Essie so they could hear the discussion.

"Essie, if you must know, there's another reason that I was upset and that possibly led to my collapse," said Bob.

"It's what I told you he wanted to tell me about after Bingo that night, Essie," added Evelyn.

"I explained this to my wife . . ." and he smiled again at Evelyn as using this word obviously still felt new to his lips.  "Something happened the day of the Bingo game that caused me a huge shock. I didn't know what to do about it and I was debating how—or if—I should even tell Evelyn.  I eventually realized that I had to tell her and I intended to tell her after Bingo—then I collapsed and wasn't able to explain the problem until just today."

"And, Essie, it really isn't a problem," said Evelyn.  "At least I don't think it's a problem."

Essie wasn't certain if this "problem" Bob was speaking of related to the letter from Ben Jericho or the newspaper clipping about Violet Hendrickson's DUI.  She chose one.

"Could it have something to do with Violet?" she asked.

"Violet?" asked Bob.  "Oh, my!  You must mean . . . Essie, are you talking about her DUI conviction?"

"Is that what you're talking about?" asked Essie.

"No," said Bob, "I don't know how you know about that.  One of the Board members here asked me to look into Violet's past—and I had hired an investigator to check into her background.  Yes, Violet does have a rather checkered past . . ."

"I'd say," noted Essie.

"I don't know how you know about all of that, Essie," said Bob.

"Essie knows a lot of things," called out Marjorie from behind her friend.

"She's very smart," added Opal.  Fay smiled and nodded.

"Anyway," continued Bob, "my investigator checked into Violet's background.  After all, she is the Director of the facility where I live—and where my wife lives.  I want that person to be qualified and ethical.  My investigator found quite a few anomalies."

"Like she's had several different identities to hide her DUI's," said Essie.

"You are a whippersnapper, Essie," said Bob, shaking his head.

"Yes," he said.  "We found out all of that.  But, Essie, all of that happened years and years ago.  Violet was named the Director here over twelve years ago—long after her DUI's and her identity changing had occurred.  And the identity changing occurred to cover up each of the DUIs.  There was some scandal in how she was appointed, but my investigators never found anything to indicate that she was culpable in securing her position.  And since she's served in an exemplary fashion for the last twelve years—including not only making Happy Haven financially solvent—which it hadn't been before—but making it actually profitable, I personally see no reason to doubt her capabilities."

"You mean you're not stressed out because of Violet," said Essie.

"Nope," answered Bob. He looked around. Both Violet and Sue were nowhere to be seen. They had obviously exited with the majority of the residents. Bob and Evelyn were now relatively alone in the lobby with Essie, Fay, Marjorie, and Opal. Phyllis stood behind the counter out of hearing range.

"So," said Essie, "it was something else altogether that caused you so much stress that you collapsed at Bingo?"

"Yup," said Bob, beginning to sound more and more like John Wayne. At that moment, the main door opened and in walked a man whom Essie (and her three compatriots) recognized immediately. Ben Jericho strode towards Essie who was sitting behind her walker in the center of the lobby.

"Miss Essie!" he called. When he reached her side, he glanced over to the couple seated on the sofa. "Mr. Weiderley?" he asked.

"That's me," said Bob, reaching out his hand to the man. "Ben Jericho, I presume."

"Yes," said Jericho, as he shook Bob's hand.

"My Lord," said Bob, as he looked over at Evelyn and then back at the man standing in front of him. "You look just like Julia."

Essie gulped. She felt a shiver run up and down her back.

"Mr. Weiderley," repeated Jericho.

"I guess you might as well call me Bob," said Bob, "or—Dad— if you want to. But, I understand if you don't want to do that."

"Uh, Bob," said Jericho, "I don't know what to say. It's been like pulling teeth to discover where you were . . ."

"You went fishing, Bob," said Essie.

"Oh?" said Bob, laughing and glancing again at Evelyn. "That's what they call lying in a coma nowadays!"

"A coma!" cried Jericho.

"Yes, Ben—if I may call you Ben," said Bob, "and if anyone is the cause of that coma," he said as he looked pointedly at Essie, "I guess it would be you, Ben."

"Me?"

"Yes, it was your letter," said Bob, "your letter explaining that you are my son that sent me into a tailspin and evidently landed me on the floor."

"I'm so sorry," said Ben Jericho, kneeling in front of the older man.

"Now, hey," said Bob, motioning for Ben to get up. "It's not as if you intentionally tried to cause it."

"I didn't," said Ben. "I thought approaching you by letter first would be the best—in case you didn't want to have anything to do with me. But I just couldn't wait. I was so excited to meet you. When my Mom told me about you right before she died, I knew I had to find you. I've been trying to track you down ever since."

"I've been doing some tracking too," said Bob. "I have some investigators myself. So, as soon as I came out of my coma, I had them look into you and your company—this Medilogicos. Quite a place you have there, Ben."

"He's the Donald Trump of medical softeners," said Essie, nodding.

"Indeed he is!" agreed Bob, and he and Evelyn laughed together.

"I just want you to know, Bob," added Ben Jericho, "that you will not have to worry about your care—if you chose to stay here. I have the financial resources to assist you and I will."

"I do appreciate that, Ben," said Bob, chuckling, but I don't believe I'll need any help. I think Evelyn and I will be just fine."

"Evelyn?" asked Ben.

"Yes," said Bob. "Ben, meet your new stepmother, Evelyn Cudahy Weiderley."

"Wow!" said Ben. "Instant family!"

"Maybe not the least stressful way to acquire a family," noted Bob, "but still a joyous one!" Evelyn opened her arms and both men folded inside them as she hugged them tightly.

Essie turned and gestured to her three friends who were standing behind her gawking at the reunion scene taking place before them.

"I think we'd better leave them alone," said Essie to her gang. The women nodded in agreement and got in line behind Essie as they headed out towards the family room.

"I'm exhausted!" said Essie. "All that sleuthing has worn me out!"

"But, Essie," argued Marjorie, "all of the plots that you thought were afoot weren't."

"Yes, Essie," agreed Opal. "Ben Jericho wasn't a scam artist. Sue Barber wasn't a poisoner. Violet Hendrickson . . ."

"Was a drunk driver!" said Essie.

"And did change her identity three times," added Opal.

"But she didn't do anything to harm Bob," challenged Marjorie.

*And Evelyn certainly doesn't seem to be out to get Bob's money. She seems genuinely in love with him*, thought Essie.

"So she does," agreed Essie.

"So after all," said Marjorie, "all of our detecting work was to no avail."

"What?" cried Essie. "To no avail? This was the most fun I've ever had!"

All four of the ladies laughed together and squeezed their walkers and wheelchair as close as possible for a big group hug.

# Epilogue

*"With mirth and laughter let old wrinkles come."*
—William Shakespeare

Later at dinner at Essie's table—because it was obviously Essie's table—the four women rehashed the day's developments.

"Miss Essie," gushed Santos as he delivered tossed salads to all four ladies. "Is it not the best wonderful news about Mr. Bob and Miss Evelyn?" A big lock of hair fell over his forehead and he pushed it back quickly.

"It certainly is!" agreed Essie, and in her self-deprecating manner she didn't even mention her own involvement in the event.

Santos zipped off to the kitchen with an even livelier skip to his step than usual.

"I guess love is in the air," noted Marjorie.

"You mean Santos?" asked Opal. "Who's he in love with?"

"I mean that Bob and Evelyn's romance has inspired everyone. The whole staff is just beaming," replied Marjorie.

Opal noticed Essie's less than joyful expression. "What is it, Essie?" she asked.

"Aren't you as excited for Bob and Evelyn as the rest of us?" queried Marjorie.

"Of course I am," responded Essie. "It's just hard to accept that none of those people who I thought posed a threat—did." She pouted and ran her fork around her salad plate in concentric circles.

"Essie!" cried Marjorie, "You should be thrilled that it turned out that the suspects you suspected don't deserve your . . . suspicion."

"After all, Essie," argued Opal, "the people you suspected were
. . . are friends and staff here at Happy Haven. It would be terrible
if one of them turned out to be guilty of attempted murder."

"Or worse," added Marjorie.

"What's worse than attempted murder?" asked Essie, slamming
down her utensil and sneering at Marjorie.

"Uh . . . actual murder," suggested Marjorie.

Santos whizzed back and quickly removed their salad plates.

"Hey, wait a minute!" cried out Essie. "I haven't finished with
that!"

"My apologies, Miss Essie," replied Santos, with a gracious
bow accompanying his apology as he replaced her salad plate.

"No," she shrugged. "Take it away."

"As you wish, Miss Essie." He retreated again.

"Really, Essie," continued Opal, "you're acting as if you've lost
your best friend. You should be thrilled that everything turned out
so well!"

"I know. I know," agreed Essie. "It's just that all that sleuthing
really got my juices going.

"Which juices would those be?" asked Marjorie with a sly
gleam in her eye.

"Not those juices, Marjorie," snapped Essie, "get your mind out
of the gutter."

"It wasn't in the gutter," said Marjorie, "it was in the toilet."
She laughed out loud and quickly covered her mouth with her
hand.

"My creative juices," clarified Essie.

"I understand, Essie," said Opal, in support. "Helping Bob and
trying to figure out what happened to him gave all of us something
important to do."

"For a change," added Marjorie.

"Yes," said Essie. "People think all we old people are good for
is just sitting around making macramé baskets and playing
solitaire."

"I hate solitaire," noted Opal.

"That's not the point," explained Essie. "They think just because we're old that we can't contribute to society or accomplish anything important on our own."

"Well, they're wrong!" exclaimed Marjorie.

"They certainly are," agreed Essie. "When three—I mean four," and she smiled at Fay who was actually awake and apparently listening to her diatribe, "ladies put their minds together—there's no telling what they can do!"

"And we almost did it!" said Marjorie.

"Almost!" said Essie, "We did do it! If it hadn't been for us, I don't think Bob and his son would ever have found each other."

"Maybe not," said Opal, "we certainly did keep that fire burning, didn't we?"

"We did!" agreed Marjorie. "And Evelyn! You supported her, Essie. I know she appreciated that."

"I tried," said Essie, nodding.

"And, of course," noted Opal, "if it hadn't been for us, the escapades of Violet Hendrickson would never have seen the light of day."

"Those escapades saw the light of day—for a brief moment—and are now back in the dark," said Essie, "which is where they need to stay—according to Bob. Are we agreed to that?"

The women all nodded. Santos arrived with their entrees—spaghetti.

"Spaghetti is so much fun to eat!" declared Marjorie. "Like rolling worms around your fork!"

"Yuck! Marjorie!" scowled Opal.

"Ladies," said Essie, in her calming voice. "Let's behave!" They all dug into the heavenly marinara sauce that the kitchen had lovingly created.

"Yum!" said Fay suddenly.

"Fay!" exclaimed Essie. "It's nice to hear from you!"

"Yum! Yum!" repeated Fay.

"A veritable monologue," reported Opal. "What's brought about her loquaciousness?"

"I don't know," shrugged Essie.    They nibbled in silence except for a few moans of ecstasy over the sauce.

"Essie, I was thinking," said Marjorie after most of the plates were almost clean.    "I was thinking that our wonderful kitchen might enjoy putting together a post-wedding reception for Bob and Evelyn."

"Marjorie!" replied Essie, "What a wonderful idea!   What do you say, Opal?"

"I agree," said the tall, somber looking member of the group. "Let's suggest it to them."

"We'll need a theme," said Marjorie.

"A theme?" asked Essie.

"Yes!" explained Marjorie, "every wedding these days is built around a theme.  Don't you watch David Tutero?  You could have a seaside theme, or a roses theme, or an all black and white theme . . . or. . . or any kind of theme you want."

"You'd want a theme that Bob and Evelyn would like," noted Opal.

"Yes.  What do you suppose that would be?" asked Marjorie.

"I know!" shouted Essie, holding up her hand.

"What?" asked Marjorie.

"Given recent events, I suggest a Bingo theme!" she exclaimed.

"How perfect!" cried Marjorie.

"With Bingo cards as placemats," offered Opal.

"And we can throw Bingo tiles instead of confetti!" added Marjorie.

And Sue Barber can read the wedding vows like a Bingo caller," said Opal.

"Only one thing we don't want," cautioned Essie.

"What?" asked Marjorie and Opal together.

"We don't want the groom to pass out if he wins!"

Santos rushed back to their table and presented each lady with her own goblet of hot fudge sundae.

"Yum!" squeaked Fay again.

"She's getting downright talkative," said Opal.

"It just goes to show what being among friends will do for you!" said Essie.

Santos bent down and whispered in Essie's ear. "Miss Essie, can I talk to you? I'm afraid that someone is trying to sabotage me. In the kitchen, Miss Essie. I thought maybe you could help . . ."

And, of course, she could . . . and she would.

**Recipes from the Happy Haven Kitchen**

*Chocolate Pudding Cake*

| | |
|---|---|
| 1 cup flour | 1/4 cup granulated sugar |
| 3 TB cocoa | 2 tsp baking powder |
| 1/4 teaspoon salt | 1/2 cup milk |
| 2 TB vegetable oil | 1 tsp vanilla |
| 3/4 cup brown sugar | 1/4 cup cocoa |
| 1 and 3/4 cups boiling water | |

Heat oven to 350°. In a bowl, mix together flour, sugar, 3 TB cocoa, baking powder and salt. With a fork, mix in milk, oil and vanilla. Spread the batter evenly in a lightly buttered 9-inch square baking pan. Combine brown sugar and 1/4 cup cocoa; sprinkle over batter. Slowly pour boiling hot water over batter and brown sugar-cocoa mix. Bake cake for 40 minutes. Let cake stand for 5 minutes. Spoon into dessert dishes or cut into squares. Top cake with ice cream or whipped topping.

*Croque Monsieurs*

| | |
|---|---|
| 8 slices white bread | 4 ounces butter, softened |
| 4 slices ham | 4 slices gruyere cheese |
| 2 eggs, slightly beaten | 1 TB water |
| salt | fresh  black pepper |

Spread bread slices with some softened butter, make 4 sandwiches, each with one slice of ham and one slice of cheese. Press them firmly together.   Beat eggs with the water, add the salt and pepper to taste, and dip sandwiches into the egg mixture, coating all sides well.   Heat rest of butter in a heavy skillet.   When melted, fry sandwiches for about 5-8 minutes, turning once.   Serve immediately.   You may place  Croque Monsieurs into a buttered baking pan and bake in a moderately hot oven—350°—turning once, for about 10 to 15 minutes.

*Bingoed* is the first book in the Essie Cobb, Senior Sleuth, mystery series by Patricia Rockwell. Ms. Rockwell is also the author of the Pamela Barnes acoustic mystery series which includes, *Sounds of Murder*, *FM for Murder*, and *Voice Mail Murder*.

Patricia Rockwell has spent most of her life teaching. Her Bachelors' and Masters' degrees are from the University of Nebraska in Speech, and her Ph.D. is from the University of Arizona in Communication. She was on the faculty at the University of Louisiana at Lafayette for thirteen years, retiring in 2007. Her publications are extensive, with over 20 peer-reviewed articles in scholarly journals, several textbooks, and a research volume published by Edwin Mellen Press. In addition, she served for eight years as editor of the *Louisiana Communication Journal*. Her research focuses primarily on deception, sarcasm, and vocal cues.

Dr. Rockwell is presently living in Aurora, Illinois, with her husband Milt, also a retired educator. The couple has two adult children.

9289510R0

Made in the USA
Charleston, SC
29 August 2011